SUPERGHOST

SCOTT COLE

SuperGhost originally published in slightly different form in 2014

Cover Art and Interior Layout by Scott Cole

Black T-Shirt Books Logo by Chris Enterline

Also By Scott Cole

Triple Axe

Slices: Tales of Bizarro and Absurdist Horror

"Okay, now take a deep breath, and close your eyes. Bite down on this."

The electric hum in the air let Dr. Rains know that things were working properly. Years of toil had led him to this—years of trial and error, compounded by years of pain and ostracism. In a few more minutes, he would be heading back to the lab with an important addition to his collection.

Sparks popped from the contraption, a rigid tube wrapped around the space the bodybuilder's lower left leg used to occupy until the freak rowing machine accident two months before. The lights in the room flickered briefly, then the buzzing sounds dissipated.

"There. You can open your eyes now." The doctor removed the bite-bar from his patient's mouth. "How do you feel?"

"Uh, pretty good, I guess. I can't feel my leg. Well, you know what I mean."

The doctor smiled. "See? I told you it would work."

"Yeah. Yeah, I guess so. Wow. Thanks."

"Not at all. Now maybe you can get back to a relatively normal life. This phantom limb syndrome you've been living with since the accident, and all the associated pain and discomfort, should now be a thing of the past." The doctor spoke in a calm and comforting voice. The bodybuilder trusted him. "Now, I'm going to prescribe some medication for you. In fact, I've brought along a sample packet. I suggest you start on it right now, just to head off any potential side effects from the start. I'll wait with you just to make sure everything goes down smoothly."

The bodybuilder pushed himself up in his chair. "Side effects? You didn't say anything about side effects."

"Yes, I know. But, you have to realize that any medical procedure has its risks. You understand that, don't you?"

The bodybuilder nodded.

"Good. Here, then. Open wide. Mmm-hmm. There, good."

The bodybuilder swallowed the solution, and tried to form the words for his next question, but the poison was fast-acting. Instead, he slumped back down into his chair and quivered violently as his flesh dissolved. His bones and organs fizzed inside him, bubbling out from his orifices and the cracks that formed as his skin broke apart and fell to pieces. Small trails of steam rose from him, and soon he was just a puddle of pink, foam-edged soup on the chair, dripping to the floor, dressed in a pair of jeans and a tank top.

The room was silent. Dr. Rains took a deep breath, then began preparing the rest of the equipment he had brought with him.

"It's so wonderful that even without one of your limbs, you were still able to stay so fit. Those core muscles, especially, are going to come in very handy."

Darren reached for the cup of water, knowing he was unable to grab it. Trina, not thinking, had set it down to his right. She had even brushed past his empty sleeve.

Nearly everyone else in the circle had coffee, but Darren had opted for water. The sensations he'd been experiencing lately made him antsy enough. He didn't need to pour caffeine on his anxiety. He wondered why they didn't have decaf available.

The doctors called it "phantom limb syndrome". As they had explained to Darren, it happens to people who lose limbs, as well as those born without them. Sometimes there is pain or discomfort, other times it's just the sensation of having what isn't actually there.

"Thanks," Darren whispered to Trina. "But, uh... maybe next time you could set the cup down to my left?" He smirked and then smiled. "You know I'm a pillar of the community, right? I literally helped build this city."

"Oh. Crap. Sorry, hon," Trina said, realizing her mistake. She squeezed her lower lip between her teeth, and ran a hand through the blue-dyed streak in her otherwise black, short-cropped hair.

"I mean, I feel a little uncomfortable being here in the first place," he said. "No need to make me look silly on top of that, right?" Darren stuck the tip of his tongue out the corner of his mouth and crossed his eyes.

Trina blushed and smiled, then moved the cup of water around to Darren's opposite side.

All these years later, he still wasn't used to the fact that things were different than they once were. That his body wasn't the way it used to be. That it never would be the same again. He still found himself reaching for things, like glasses of water, with his right arm. The one that wasn't there anymore.

The accident might have taken his arm, but it hadn't taken his determination. In the years since, he had learned to adapt and cope, although his current lack of employment was still a regular challenge. His job skills were limited, and with only one arm, he was considered a liability in the construction business. Workers generally needed both arms to operate a crane, or a forklift, or even a jackhammer.

The insurance settlement ensured that he had enough money to survive. But that wasn't enough for Darren. He wanted to work, to contribute to something. He wanted to build.

"Oh, I meant to tell you," Darren whispered. "I was going through some things I had in storage, and I found all my old building blocks from when I was a kid. A lot of the paint's chipped away, but they're still pretty cool."

"Nice," said Trina. "Tell me about it later, though.

We're here for a reason, you know." She motioned toward the center of the circle with her eyes.

Darren had been interested in construction even as a small child. It began with brightly-colored wooden blocks. Then he moved on to Lincoln Logs, Legos, and Erector Sets. When his parents cleaned up his toys at the end of any given night, he was devastated by the fact that they had disassembled his work.

As he grew up, other opportunities presented themselves, but he chose to stick with what he loved to do. There was just something about building with raw materials.

So when his right arm was torn off by a drunken farmer driving a stolen bulldozer the wrong way down a one-way city street, Darren was destroyed, both physically and emotionally. But he was still able to see the irony in being a construction worker with structural damage. He always kept his sense of humor.

"Yeah, yeah," he said.

"Hey, we're giving this a chance, right?" Trina said. "The doctor said a support group could really help. We haven't been here five minutes and already you're grumbling."

Trina was generally the shy, quiet type. And here she was, pushing Darren to open up and talk to complete strangers. Darren found that a little amusing. He went along with it, though. He had trouble telling her no.

She was a true friend.

She also worked in the test kitchen of the Happee Freeze Ice Cream Company downtown, which didn't hurt. Every time she visited, she brought at least one specialty pint along with her, often something no one outside the company had tried yet.

Tonight, there was a pint of Chocolate Coriander Crumble waiting for him. He didn't even know what coriander was, but anything containing the word chocolate piqued his interest. Of course, she had made him come to this support group session before he was allowed to taste it.

Twenty people sat in a circle in the center of the high school classroom, desks separating them as comfort barriers.

"Welcome, Darren," the group said in unison. Darren nodded.

He listened to a guy named Wilson talk about losing an arm and a leg in Afghanistan. There was a woman named Bea who had lost both feet to diabetes. And there was an older lady named Ms. Ramirez, who claimed to have lost her leg to a truck full of celery at some sort of vegetable-themed festival down by the waterfront. There was even a guy named Dick who claimed to have lost his penis to a newspaper box.

They talked about their accidents, and their triumphs, like teaching themselves how to drive without feet, how to tie shoes with only three fingers, how to write with a previously non-dominant hand.

Two guys in trucker hats on the opposite side of the room laughed while making masturbatory motions with their left hands. One of them slurred something with a Southern twang in his voice, then hiccupped and fell off his chair. His one-armed buddy helped him stand, then excused both of them, saying they had another meeting to attend, down the hall.

Darren chuckled, and glanced back at Trina, who

was blushing again. She pushed his shoulder, her way of telling him to shut up and turn back around.

"Sorry to keep coming back to this," someone in the group said, "but...*a newspaper box?*"

"Motherfucker!" screamed Michelle, the sound of her voice reverberating off the walls of her apartment.

"I want this just as bad as you do, you know." Dr. Rains was doing his best to console his patient. "I understand your frustration. I really do. But getting upset and hurling insults in my direction ultimately does neither of us any good."

"I disagree," said Michelle. "I feel a little better already." She grabbed the sides of her wheelchair, and spun away from the doctor, to face her kitchen doorway. "What's with your get-up today anyway? You cold? I can turn the heat up if you want to take your overcoat off." She spun back around to face him. "Or maybe you're just embarrassed about that ridiculous neon orange lab coat you have on underneath?" The doctor looked down at himself, momentarily taken aback by his patient's comment. "And goggles? This is in-home therapy. We're just talking."

"All right, Ms. Mayfair. We're not meeting today to discuss my attire."

"And just for the record, I doubt you want this as bad as me. You still have your legs." She rolled herself to the other side of the room, toward the curio cabinet containing the majority of her medals—some of them Olympic, most of them gold—and turned back toward Dr. Rains.

"Fair enough. But listen, I do want to help you. Truly. Your legs are gone. That's enough trauma for anyone. Especially for someone who depended on them—someone whose identity was tied to them." He glanced over his shoulder, toward Michelle's "wall of fame." He paused for a moment, and took in the dozens of plaques, the framed photos with other famous athletes, celebrities, and politicians. He didn't recognize all the faces, but he knew most of them.

"Bullshit," said Michelle.

"There's no need for you to be in pain, or to be experiencing these types of sensations. Even when your phantom limbs don't cause you physical discomfort, I know that it hurts you up here." Dr. Rains tapped the side of his perfectly round, hairless head with the tip of an index finger.

Michelle stopped her torrent of expletives. She reached up and ran fingers through her own hair, wavy, thick and dark brown, almost as if to flaunt it in front of the bald man. But she was listening.

"Look, I get it. You're not who you once were. I realize there may be feelings of inadequacy—or that you may feel, for lack of a better word, *incomplete*. I get that. I really do. Because this is what I do. I'm here to help."

Michelle glanced downward. She could still feel her

legs, strong and solid, but she was still learning how to cope with the fact that they were no longer there.

"Now, of course we can simply continue this course of talk-it-through therapy. That's fine, if that's what you want. I'm happy to keep visiting you." The doctor paused. "But it seems to me—and please tell me if you disagree—"

"Oh, don't worry," Michelle interrupted. "I will."

"Yes, dear. I'm certain of that. It seems to me our discussions are only doing so much good. At a certain point, we tend to hit a wall."

"Ain't that the truth." She paused, as did Rains. "It's just frustrating, you know? I mean, we've been at this for how long now? I'm fine some days, but other times...I dunno. It's agony."

"That's exactly what I was getting to. You see, I believe I do have another way to help. It's a procedure—"

"Ohhh no. No way. I am not going under the friggin' knife again."

"Ms. Mayfair. Michelle. Listen to me. It's nothing like that. It's a procedure, yes, but it's not surgery. We can do this right here in your home. No knives. Nothing invasive. Easy. No muss, no fuss."

Michelle cocked her head.

"Now, I will admit, it is a bit on the experimental side. But that's simply because it's a process I've invented. And technically—*technically*—no one else in the medical community has seen this yet, although I expect that will change soon enough. I just need to get through a few more rounds of field testing, and—"

"Yeah, well, I'm not so sure..." Michelle slumped a bit.

"Come, now. You left that support group behind in favor of these one-on-one sessions, right? Why did you do that? Because you saw something in me. Isn't that right? You saw something that made you trust me, trust that I could get you through some rough times. And you haven't gone back to the group, have you? You haven't cast me aside. So you must still trust that I can help."

The doctor paused. Michelle didn't say anything.

"Now, when I say this procedure is experimental, I realize that makes it sound a bit scary. I suppose I should have chosen a better term. But there's really nothing to be concerned about. After all, this is designed to help you."

"I get that," Michelle said. "But don't you have to get this sort of thing approved by the FDA or something? I mean, the whole experimental thing...I don't think—"

"Did I mention it would be completely free?"

"I'm sorry?" Michelle perked up.

"Oh yes! I couldn't think of taking someone's hard-earned money. Not if they're helping me with the field tests. Helping science."

"So, what's involved?"

"Tell you what," the doctor said as he looked at the time on his wrist. "Let me stop back tomorrow, and we'll go through everything. I have a dinner meeting I need to get to, across town. But tomorrow, I'll tell you every detail, answer every question."

Michelle nodded, and watched from her wheelchair as the doctor walked to her door and let himself out.

"See? That wasn't so terrible, was it?" asked Trina in the car on the way back to Darren's apartment.

"We never did get to the bottom of how exactly that one guy lost his junk, did we?" Darren said, smiling. Trina rolled her eyes. "Anyway, where's my ice cream?"

"Back at your place. I dumped it in your freezer when I picked you up. Oh, you didn't see me?" Trina said.

"Goddammit. You mean the Chocolate Cori-whatever was there the whole time?" Darren said with faux-annoyance. "I coulda skipped that meeting?"

"Nope. We had a deal," said Trina. "And you're going to the next one too. Thursday night."

"Hmm...we'll see. My Thursdays are worth two pints."

Trina pulled her ancient hatchback up to Darren's place, walked him inside, then presented him with a bowl of ice cream before leaving for the night.

"I have tomorrow off. I'll stop by and you can let me know what you think of that one," she said.

Darren continued to act playfully annoyed, but smiled the second the door clicked shut.

Later that night, Darren dreamt of creepy-crawly things. Bugs. Spiders. Cockroaches. Slimy worm-like creatures with millions of legs, and other things with tiny hairs to tickle his flesh. It was claustrophobia, with agitators.

The sensation was still with him when he woke up an hour and a half later. It was as if he had fallen asleep on his arm, causing the pins and needles effect that his mother used to say was just as bad as fingernails on a chalkboard.

He had dealt with this in the past, but it was getting worse lately—bad enough that it would wake him in the middle of the night. It was an itch he couldn't scratch, a rash without a salve.

He stayed awake through the dark hours, coping. He tried to occupy himself with TV in an attempt to take his mind off the itchy phantom pain, but it only worked to a small extent. He tried other things too, like rubbing a hairbrush on his shoulder stub, but that only relieved a few seconds worth of his agony.

He walked to the bedroom closet.

A doctor had once convinced him to buy a mirror box for home therapy, the idea being that he would stick his left arm in one side, and his phantom arm in the other, and by looking at the mirror that divided them and seeing the reflection of his existing arm, it would help connect some of the dots in his brain, and he would see a visual representation of the movements that he felt.

He never quite understood how that was supposed to help. Several doctors had recommended it to him, saying it had been a boon to other patients, but Darren was convinced it was all just a scam to sell these contraptions. The doctors who recommended them probably got a percentage of each unit they unloaded.

He dug his mirror box out of the closet anyway, desperate for anything that might help him get through the night.

It didn't work, but at least his mind had been somewhat occupied during his fifteen minute search for the thing. Of course, now there was a pile of clothes on the floor in front of the closet that needed to be put back away. He'd deal with that in the morning.

Eventually, hours later, after another bowl of ice cream, Darren fell back to sleep in front of the TV.

The next afternoon, Dr. Rains returned to Michelle Mayfair's home.

"And how are you today, Ms. Mayfair?"

"How do you think?" Michelle responded. "I'm a former Olympian who now serves weird ice cream in a wheelchair, from behind a counter I can barely see over, in a corner shop in the worst part of town."

"Yes, well..."

"I used to hang out with celebrities, you know? I used to get invited to big time galas, rub elbows with the elite, eat lobster with politicians..."

"I know," said Rains, cutting her off. "Sometimes life takes a turn for the worse. But with any luck, after today, things will take another turn, for the better."

Rains wheeled something through the door, and began to tell Michelle a bit more about the impending procedure. His explanation wasn't too in depth, but he used enough technical jargon that it sounded impressive.

"I call it the Phantom Zapper!" he finally announced, running a hand down the front of his lime green lab coat, the front of which was exposed by his open overcoat. He was clearly pleased with himself.

"That's the name? You should've told me that when you were here yesterday. We could've saved you a trip!" Michelle yelled. "You couldn't come up with anything better?"

"What do you mean?" Rains asked.

"Well, it's a bit silly, don't you think?" Michelle shifted in her chair, and rubbed her stumps with her hands. The itchy sensations she experienced from time to time had been getting worse. They had been particularly bad that morning, and the pain was beginning to intensify again. It felt like a swarm of flies had replaced her legs, with occasional electric shocks.

"Err...no. I don't think so at all," Rains said. "What would you call it?"

"Something better than that. A five-year-old could've come up with 'Phantom Zapper'. Shit, a spoonful of alphabet soup could come up with a better name than that."

"Everyone is entitled to their own opinion. Now, let me show you how this works—"

"Hold on," Michelle interrupted. "Let's just think about this a second. I was okay with this whole thing—I mean, you convinced me, when I thought we were talking about a serious, medical procedure. But now you walk in with a friggin' who-knows-what on a hand truck, hidden under a dirty sheet, and you're calling it a 'Zapper'? I don't think so."

"If you'll just let me demonstrate—"

"No, no. Just hold on. I don't even wanna see the thing if that's what we're calling it. We need to come up with a new name. Something a little more dignified. Or at least not so...childlike."

"Well, I had another name, originally." Dr. Rains said, his voice a bit lower now. Michelle didn't respond—just waited, bracing herself. "I was going to call it..."

"Come on, spit it out."

"I was going to call it...Dr. Rains' Ghostacular Ghost-Grabber."

"Get the fuck out."

Michelle grabbed the wheels of her chair and rolled herself toward the doctor. She was serious—she wanted his ass on the other side of her door.

"Please, Ms. Mayfair," he said, raising his hands up in front of his body. "You know I want to help you."

Michelle stopped her wheelchair and sat silently for a moment, staring at the doctor. She felt as if her legs were vibrating, even though they were long gone.

"The world's a horrible place," he said. "I know this. Believe me, I've been dealt lousy cards more often than I like to admit. I may have my limbs intact, but I've felt pain. I've been treated unfairly, felt the hate and derision of others, from elementary school through medical school to the present-day scientific community. I know how the world can chew you up and spit you out. But the trick, you see, is to pick up the pieces, put yourself back together, so to speak, and charge forward. Show those bastards what you're made of."

Michelle dropped her gaze to her lap.

"That's why I do what I do," Rains said. "Let me

help."

Michelle stared at her stubs and thought about her life. She sighed as the pain subsided for a moment. Then she got hit with another shock, almost as painful as when her legs were originally torn off. She made a sound that startled the doctor, then she took a deep breath and rubbed her stumps again.

"Okay," she said, a minute later. She blinked, and a tear fell from the corner of her left eye. "Let's just pretend this thing doesn't have a name."

"Apparently there's a big science thing happening down at the convention center this weekend," Trina said, staring at Darren's computer screen while trying to organize some of the mess on his desk. "Did you know about that?"

"Yeah, I saw something on the news," Darren said. "What was it? *Science Now!*, right?"

"That's the one."

"What are you doing with my desk anyway? And shouldn't you be at work?"

"Day off," Trina said. "Didn't I mention it? They're installing this new giant freezer. It's crazy, actually. I swear it's practically the size of a football stadium. Speaking of which, *your* freezer is now officially packed with Happee Freeze ice cream. No more room for new stuff until you eat what you've got."

"You trying to fatten me up?" Darren said with his typically flirty smirk.

"One pint at a time, my friend. I brought you some super-new ones: Raspberry Lime Cocoa Coconut and Thai

Peanut Curry."

"Curry? Curry ice cream?" Darren stuck his tongue out. "Okay, so maybe I won't get fat on that. Because, you know, it sounds disgusting."

Trina chuckled. "Give it a try. It's delicious," she said. "And maybe this time give me something more than 'Eww, I don't like coriander in my chocolate unless it's peanut butter coriander'."

"You know, I'm not sure how I feel about being your little frozen treat guinea pig, darlin'," Darren said. "How do I know you're not cooking up some weird poison in that little test kitchen of yours?"

"Yup, that's why I've been hanging out by your side all this time. I just wanted to build you back up so I could take you out...with ice cream." Trina laughed. Darren cocked an eyebrow.

"So anyway, why are you here again?" he asked.

"No real reason. Just thought I'd check in with you. Plus, my internet's down at home, and I need to send a few emails."

"See? Poison ice cream and high-speed internet access. I knew that's the real reason you kept showing up," Darren said. Then, suddenly, he winced. *"Ahh! Dammit!"*

"What's wrong?" Trina stood up and moved closer to Darren.

"Just this stupid ghost arm. Feels like I just got hit by lightning. It's been driving me crazy lately. Last night was rough."

"Do you need something?" Trina asked.

"Yeah, can you amputate a phantom limb?" He was frustrated, but not angry—not at her, at least.

"Actually, I was just going to suggest we go to this science convention thing. Maybe there's someone there who can help."

"Come on, Trina. I already went to that support group last night. Didn't help a damn thing."

"Well, maybe if you had opened your mouth, it would have. You just sat there. The idea of a support group is to talk to the other people there. Make friends. Share experiences."

"Oh, you're one to talk, aren't you? You didn't say a word either. You never do."

"Yeah, well, it wasn't a shy person support group, was it? Look, I'm just trying to help you out here; I want you to be happy. And you don't seem to want to help yourself."

"Nobody's got the solution for this. At least nothing that takes."

"Well, that's why we're trying different things, isn't it? Maybe one of these scientists can do something. There are top people coming in from all over the world for this."

"No way," said Darren.

"Fine. Whatever. Then at least promise me you'll go back to the support group tomorrow night."

Silence.

"Okay?" asked Trina, raising her eyebrows at Darren. "What do you say?"

"Fine," said Darren. "How 'bout a bowl of ice cream for lunch?"

"If that's what it takes to seal the deal. What kind do you want?"

"Surprise me." Darren shifted position and threw

his legs up on the couch. Trina walked to the kitchen, clanged a few dishes around, and returned a minute later.

"Here you go. Bubble Gummi Bear Swirl." She handed off the bowl and picked her bag up off the couch. "I've got errands to run. We'll talk later, though. And I'll definitely be seeing you tomorrow night."

"Mmmhmm," he said in response, as Trina mussed his hair. A few seconds later, she gave him a wink from the doorway, then pulled the door shut.

Darren sniffed the bowl of ice cream and wrinkled his nose.

Dr. Rains' invention sat upright, just inside the door of Michelle's apartment, on a hand truck. It was a beat up, rusty old thing that dinged like a bell with every turn of the tires—tires which no longer held air very well.

The hand truck was practically an heirloom at this point, a thing held onto for nostalgic reasons more than its usability.

It got the job done, though.

The doctor had used it to transport those elephant parts all those years ago, prior to building the Elephant Train.

He had used it to transport the lab equipment he would later use in his creation of the Neverending Mango, something he had come up with in an effort to rid the world of famine. Unfortunately he had not anticipated the mango turning on humans and devouring them instead.

He had also used the hand truck to deliver his Automatic Change-Paint into stores. Sadly, that invention had to be scrapped as well, when people could no longer find their homes.

And he never could have assembled his time machine without this piece of equipment, even if the thing had only been mildly successful, sending his subject back just five minutes, every five minutes, resulting in an endless loop that had to be relived over and over, until he managed to send a hammer back in time to collide with the subject's head at just the right moment.

Sure, there were better models of hand truck available now—ones that didn't make such a racket when they moved—but he had a lot of memories tied into this one.

Now the Phantom Zapper sat upon it, hidden beneath a drop cloth.

"Looks like those tires could use some air," Michelle said. "Need to borrow my pump?"

Dr. Rains ignored her, and removed the sheet he had draped over his invention. It looked like something out of a sci-fi movie.

It resembled a full body cast, pure white and smooth. It had been separated into various sections, though, then reassembled with metal bands, leather straps, and brass buckles. Each section of the body-shell was separate, but could be connected to the next part down the line. There was a piece for each hand, one for each forearm, one for each upper arm, a torso, a helmet, and so on. The whole thing could be used just as easily as a single section. Wires sprouted from each piece, and all ran back to a hub, a vertical metal box mounted to the back of the hand truck. It was covered with LEDs and switches, dials and gauges.

"Obviously we won't be needing the entire thing

today," the doctor explained. "But I like keeping the whole contraption together. I guess you could say I'm a completist of sorts."

Dr. Rains separated the legs from the torso, but kept the ankle and knee attachments locked in place.

"Can you come over this way now?" he asked. Michelle rolled her wheelchair over to him.

"Okay. Now, what I need you to do is place your phantoms—your legs, that is—into these. Think of it as a pair of pants. A very stiff pair of pants. Like the dry cleaner went a bit crazy with the starch."

Michelle braced herself on the armrests of her chair, and shifted her body forward a few inches. She winced, uncomfortable.

"They're really bothering me today, Doc."

"Think of sandpaper scratching that itch away. It's the last time you'll need to do it."

"Why don't you take your coat off or something? I feel like you're about to run out the door. Aren't you supposed to put the patient at ease?"

"It's a bit drafty in here," Rains said. "Don't you think? Besides, this procedure won't take long at all."

"Okay. There." Michelle grunted, then breathed a sigh of relief. "They're in."

"You're sure?"

"Of course I'm sure! What the fuck, Doc?"

"All right, all right," Dr. Rains said calmly. They were so close now. An argument could throw his entire plan out of whack. "Here. Open up, and bite down on this." He placed a metal tube wrapped in leather into Michelle's mouth sideways. "Ready?"

Michelle nodded, and closed her eyes before Rains could ask her to do so. He walked quickly back to the hand truck, where the control panel sat, at the top of the rig.

He flipped a switch, and the entire room began to hum. The sound was soft at first, then grew in intensity.

"Here we go," he said, turning a dial. The electrical hum got louder as the lights in the room dimmed, then flickered. The knee and ankle connectors on the Phantom Zapper sparked. The electrical hum turned to static. The sounds in the room intensified for another minute, and then there was a pop, and the lights came back up to full brightness. The room fell silent again.

Michelle cracked her eyes open, and loosened her jaw's grip on the tube in her mouth. A quiet moan escaped her lips.

The doctor turned the dial on the machine all the way back to zero, and flipped all the switches off, powering everything down, then approached Michelle.

"What do you feel?" he asked.

"Nothing." Michelle responded with a whisper.

"Nothing?"

"Yeah. Nothing. I can't feel my legs anymore." She smiled.

"Excellent." The doctor pressed a button on the side of each leg-shell, then undid the straps holding them in place. He packed his gear up quickly, and threw the sheet back over the contraption.

"I think it actually worked, Doc!" Michelle was amazed. Her lips lifted into a smile for the first time in a long time. She looked down, feeling nothing past the ends of her stumps.

She looked back up just in time to see Dr. Rains pull the door shut on his way out. He didn't even say goodbye.

An hour later, Dr. Rains was back at his laboratory. The building, a former warehouse, had a few smaller rooms, and two significantly larger spaces, one of which had been converted into Rains' main lab. That room, where he was examining his latest acquisitions, now confined to a large glass tank, was filled with hundreds of similar such cases. They lined the walls of the room, all the way up to the ceiling, dozens of feet above.

"Ahh, perfect. Now that's a beautiful pair of legs," he said to himself, or perhaps to the phantom limbs. They stayed afloat, hovering inside the glass box, barely visible on their own. This particular pair of legs—or rather the ghosts of them—once belonged to an elite Olympic runner. They rarely stopped moving, constantly knocking themselves against the sides of the glass, which was lined with several rows of tiny spikes, each wired with a small charge of electricity. Upon coming into contact with the spikes, the phantom limbs flickered and glowed with a soft green light, as if a flashlight had been switched on from within a patch of fog. They became solid in those moments, and unable to pass through other objects and escape their confines.

"What do you think, Sexy?" he said, turning to another, much larger glass case—the one that held his pet octopus, who had only six of his original eight arms. Rains had injected Sexy with a protein inhibitor, to keep his tentacles from regenerating.

Sexy the Sexopus seemed to nod, his entire body floating like a cloud in a watery cell. "Beautiful," he seemed to say.

"They really are stunning, aren't they? I'm almost there. Just a few more high-quality phantom arms, and I'll be ready to assemble my greatest creation yet.

"And those know-it-alls, those holier-than-thous... They'll all see just how wrong they were about me. They called me an outcast, thought my ideas were too wild, too weird. Too 'outside the box'? Ha! I'll show them! Won't I, Sexy? I'll put each one of them right *inside* a box!"

The doctor laughed out loud, then stopped abruptly and let the smile fade from his face. "Sorry. No offense, you two." Then he tossed a cloth over the glass case containing the phantom legs of the Olympian, covering it in the same way as the dozens of others in the room, and shifted focus.

He shrugged off his overcoat to reveal what he hid away from public view: his third and fourth arms—the ones he had to keep strapped down to his sides and hidden away when he went out into the world.

Stepping over to a table cluttered with glass jars and test tubes, he began following a recipe he kept in his head, combining a strange mixture of powders and liquids. He had recently decided on a name for the chemical cocktail that would enable the next, and final, phase of his grand plan. "Ghost Glue" was a bit too obvious. And so he dubbed his new concoction, his paranormal adhesive, "ConnECTO".

He chuckled quietly to himself, barely making a peep, pleased with his own special kind of madness.

Darren sat in his chair, back at the support group. Trina set a cup of water down to Darren's left, and gave him a pat on the back, right beneath his neck.

"Try talking to some of these people this time," she whispered in his ear. "It might help. Common experiences and all that."

"There were more people here the other night, weren't there?" Darren asked. Trina nodded. "Like those two drunk guys. Remember?"

"How could I forget? They were a big part of the evening's entertainment."

"Kinda funny that a phantom limb support group meeting is suddenly, uh, missing members, huh?"

Trina stifled a laugh, and pressed a knuckle into Darren's shoulder, her signature stop-being-an-ass-in-public move. Then she whispered into his ear again. "Say hi. Introduce yourself. Tell them what you've been going through. Maybe someone can give you some advice."

Darren looked back to the center of the circle, but

didn't speak. He was listening, however, and Trina hoped that might help in some small way.

A woman missing a leg and half of her pelvis was talking about her accident—something involving a carnivorous mango, if that was to be believed—when Darren started to shift in his chair.

"You okay?" Trina asked. "I know these classroom chairs weren't designed for comfort."

"I gotta go. This thing's driving me crazy. I can't focus."

Trina gathered their things quietly, and led Darren out into the hallway. She mouthed the word "sorry" to the rest of the group. A few people nodded acknowledgement.

"I'm really sorry," Darren said once they were halfway down the hall.

"It's okay," said Trina.

"It's just—*gahhh!*—this thing feels like it's on fire."

"Sorry, sweetie."

Darren continued describing the sensations as they happened. His phantom arm felt like it was being attacked by a swarm of angry insects. Cascades of biting, stinging pains swept through the space his arm used to occupy. And on top of that, there were random jolts, like lightning exploding inside the empty space. It was almost too much to bear on its own, but trying to deal with it in a classroom full of people trying to talk to each other was impossible.

They stepped through the front door of the school, and into the parking lot. One of the outdoor lamps illuminating the lot flickered on and off, and buzzed like a fly trying to get through a closed window.

"Don't you mock me!" Darren said at the lamp post,

trying his best to lighten the mood. Trina smiled, but it did nothing to quell her concern.

"Excuse me," came a voice from the darkness. Trina looked toward the sound, and spotted a man two rows away. "Are you two coming from the phantom limb group?" he asked.

Darren looked up and spotted the man. He was bald, with a round head. He wore an overcoat and goggles. The edge of what appeared to be a bright red Mandarin collar poked out from beneath his coat. He walked swiftly toward them, quickly cutting the distance between them.

"I'm sorry to disturb you both," he said. "I just wanted to make your acquaintance. I assume you were at the phantom limb meeting?"

"How—?" said Trina.

"I noticed your arm," the man said. "And I'm familiar with the schedule for that particular group." The man paused, and rubbed his hands together as if to warm them.

"O...kay," said Darren, on guard.

"My apologies, my apologies. My name is Dr. Rains. I'm a phantom limb therapist."

"Oh, I see," said Trina. "Well, the meeting's still going on. Room 215, if that's what you're looking for."

"Thank you, miss. I appreciate that," said Rains, dropping his hands back to his sides.

Trina and Darren turned toward Trina's car.

"Have you been pleased with the meetings?" Rains asked. "Are they helping?"

Darren turned around. "I'm sorry?" he said, annoyed. Trina put her hand on his elbow.

"I asked if the meetings were a help to you, and your condition," said Rains. "As I mentioned, I'm a therapist, and this sort of thing is my specialty. Actually, I'm a bit more than a therapist."

Trina slid her arm around Darren, and leaned in the direction of the car, which was only another ten feet away.

"You see, I'm not simply a doctor; I'm a scientist." Rains clasped his hands together again and stepped toward Darren and Trina. "May I give you my card?"

Darren pulled away from Trina, and felt a small phantom shock. He reached across his body to grab his shoulder stub, an effort to remind himself that that's where his arm ended. The pains he felt were phantom pains. They weren't real.

So then why did they hurt so damn much?

"Here, sir. Perhaps you'd like to give me a call sometime," Rains said, holding out a business card. "If you're having issues related to your phantom limb, and these meetings aren't working for you, please, call my office." Darren took the card and examined it.

"Come on, Darren," said Trina.

"You see, I've developed a procedure," Rains continued. "It's...well, to use a fairly apt cliché, it's rather cutting edge."

Darren looked back up at the doctor.

"Please, if you like, feel free to give me a call, and we can discuss it over the phone." Rains bowed to the couple and turned back. "Have a pleasant rest of the night," he said as he retreated between a pair of parked cars.

Trina and Darren didn't say much on the ride back to Darren's apartment. Trina came in for a few minutes to help him get settled.

"What can we do?" she said. "Have you been using your mirror box?"

"That damn thing never worked," Darren responded. "I gave it another try the other night, but it was pointless."

"So what can I do for you? Heating pad? Ice?"

"I'll be okay. It's not as bad now as it was at the meeting. I really think I just need some sleep, if I can get it."

"You sure?" Trina said. "I feel weird leaving."

"Yeah, I'll manage. I always do, one way or another," Darren said. "Why don't you go home and get some sleep yourself. You've got work tomorrow, don't you?"

"Yeah. But they're pulling us out of the kitchen tomorrow. Site visits."

"What do you mean, site visits?"

"They want us to go to some of the shops, talk to the employees, get some sense of which flavors the public really goes for. I guess it's supposed to inspire us. My boss thinks talking to the employees who talk to the customers first-hand might offer a different spin on things. Just because someone bought a scoop of Corn Cob Crunch doesn't mean they actually liked it, and would buy it again."

"Eww," said Darren, wrinkling his face. "You guys should offer free samples so people know what they're getting into."

"We do. Plus, I've got you as a pre-taster, my friend, and I know you'd never steer me wrong. Anyway, are you sure you're going to be okay tonight? I can stay if you need me too."

"No, I'll be fine," said Darren. Trina walked over and gave him a hug, which Darren held onto for an extra beat. "Go get some sleep," he said, upon letting go.

"Okay then. Any last requests?" Trina asked.

"Actually, maybe you *could* get me some ice..." Darren faked a cough. "...cream."

Trina rolled her eyes and shook her head, while Darren smiled like the Cheshire Cat. "I've created a monster," she joked.

"Nothing with corn in it."

Moments after Trina had left, Darren felt a series of explosions where his right arm used to be. Waves of cascading flames rolled up and down the void. He tried to convince himself once again that since there was no arm, there should be no pain. That the pain wasn't real, couldn't possibly exist. But he knew he was only trying to fool himself. The pain was real.

He set his bowl of ice cream down on the table, barely touched, and started pacing around the apartment. Perhaps moving would help. He wasn't completely convinced of this, but every father on the planet tells their kids to "walk off" their injuries. Maybe there was some logic to it.

The pain had been getting worse lately—far worse than he had let on to Trina. He appreciated her concern and willingness to help, but he didn't see how she could do much, and didn't want her to worry.

His stump began to itch. Darren imagined his missing limb covered with thousands, maybe millions of ants, one arm-shaped mass of bugs wriggling, crawling over each other, biting.

He thought about trying the mirror box again, but quickly abandoned the notion.

Now his phantom limb felt as if it was wrapped with baby boa constrictors, and filled with angry butterflies. Every so often, it was as if the butterflies got hit with lightning, and the snakes tightened their grip.

He grabbed his shoulder again, trying to remind himself that's where he ended, that he shouldn't feel anything past that point. It didn't work. Nothing worked.

Darren reached into his pocket and pulled out his phone. The raised printing on Dr. Rains' business card was still tacky, and caused the card to stick to his phone. He separated them and looked at the card. In the center was Rains' name and phone number surrounded by dashed-outline drawings of arms and legs. It was tacky, sure, but he certainly seemed to be a specialist in his particular field.

Darren sat down on the couch and stared at the card. He sighed.

"Thanks for stopping in," said Michelle, unenthusiastically. "Have a Happee day."

The kids didn't respond. They just walked out the door laughing, their double-scoop concoctions already starting to drip down their cones. Michelle suddenly remembered it was a weekday and wondered if the kids should have been in school instead of running around a not-so-great neighborhood getting ice cream.

She wheeled herself back behind the freezer case, the one with the curved glass front that proudly displayed a variety of unusual Happee Freeze flavors. There was no such thing as plain vanilla or chocolate at Happee Freeze. Michelle frankly didn't understand the appeal of flavors like Sesame Kale Swirl or Tahini Treat, but a job was a job, and since she was no longer an athlete with endorsement deals, she had to take what she could get.

It had been a few days since Dr. Rains had come to her apartment and performed his procedure. She didn't entirely remember him leaving that night, and hadn't been able to get a hold of him since.

The procedure had certainly worked. Ever since that night, she had been unable to feel anything past the very tops of her thighs, where the flesh ended. She was thankful for that. But she had also been overcome with the sense that something else was off. Something within her wasn't quite right. Somehow she felt incomplete.

She had felt something similar when she first lost her legs. But this was, oddly, even worse. It didn't make sense. She had what she wanted. For several days now she had been free of the pain and discomfort she thought was hindering her life.

She needed to speak with the doctor. Maybe this was a common thing. Maybe there was some sort of medication she could take, even in the short term. But Rains hadn't returned any of her calls.

She was doing her best to work through it. She needed a paycheck, and didn't normally have many customers in the afternoon anyway, so she was able to force herself into work. But to say things were okay was a bit of a stretch.

The bell hanging just above the front door dinged. "Welcome to Happee Freeze," Michelle announced, a now-automatic, nearly Pavlovian response. She looked up and saw her patron to be a woman with short hair, all black except for one streak of blue down the side. "What can I get for you today?"

"Hi," the woman said. "My name is Trina. I'm actually from Corporate."

"Shit," whispered Michelle under her breath.

"I work in the Happee Freeze test kitchen. So

technically I work in the corporate offices, but I'm not really 'Corporate'."

"Uh-huh. Am I getting fired?" Michelle asked.

"No," Trina said, laughing. "Believe me, there are days I wish I could fire someone, but sadly I don't have much power. Your job is safe, as far as I know."

"Okay, good," sighed Michelle, as she rolled out from behind the counter. "So what can I do for you?"

"Well, today's sort of a day off in the test kitchen, and they sent us out to visit some of the shops, talk to people, and try to generate some new ideas."

"Test kitchen, huh? So, what? You come up with these crazy-ass flavors?"

Trina bit her bottom lip. "That's us," she said, now baring her teeth with a wide, forced smile.

"Well, if I can make a suggestion, feel free to stop doing anything with curry. Nobody likes it."

"Really," said Trina. "I was pretty proud of that last one. I thought we really nailed the ratios. And sales on the curry flavors are great."

"Seriously. You wouldn't believe how often I have to mop this floor because people order curry-whatever and then spit it right out. And mopping isn't exactly the easiest thing in the world for someone in a chair."

"Well, I guess that's why they sent us out into the field." Trina pulled out her phone and started typing a few notes with her thumb. "So, um, if you don't mind my asking," Trina said. "How did you—"

"I was mugged," Michelle said.

"No, I meant your legs."

"Yeah, that's what I'm saying. I got held up, and

beat up. When I blacked out, they tossed me in a dumpster. Woke up in a trash truck when the door came down and bit my legs off."

"Oh my gosh," Trina gasped.

"Yeah, well, now I get all the free ice cream I want, so, you know...tradeoffs."

"Wait a second. You're Michelle Mayfair, aren't you? Wow, I watched all your races back in '08. Incredible."

"Thanks," said Michelle. "So anyway, like I said, ease up on the curry—at least for this shop. Maybe people go for that stuff in other parts of the city, but people here really prefer the sweeter stuff."

"Yeah. Thanks," said Trina. "So, can I just ask? Have you ever dealt with any phantom limb issues? A good friend of mine lost his arm, and he's been having a rough time, to say the least."

"Yeah, I did. Both legs. Until recently, that is. It was a bitch for a long time. But then I met this doctor, said he had a new procedure—"

"Oh yeah?" asked Trina. "What was his name?"

"Rains. Dr. Griffin Rains," said Michelle. "Weird dude. Always wore these colorful shirts, but never took off his overcoat."

"Wow. That's the same guy who approached my friend and I last night," Trina said.

"You met him? I've been trying to reach him for days, but he won't return my calls."

Michelle explained how Rains' procedure seemed to have been successful, and how she hadn't experienced any pain or discomfort for days, but how she was now dealing with some other feelings.

"It's not exactly depression," Michelle explained. "I don't know what you'd call it. Something's just not right. It's like, when I lost my legs, I didn't feel complete. And now my phantom limbs are gone, and I feel even less complete. Like I'm only half a person, both physically and emotionally. Something's off, so to speak."

"Huh. Well maybe my friend and I can get a hold of him," said Trina. "Although he seemed a little odd."

"Yeah, no shit," said Michelle, bobbing her head in agreement.

"Speaking of my friend...his name's Darren, by the way," Trina said. "Any chance you'd be willing to meet him? I'm worried about him, and I've been trying to get him to talk to other people with the same condition."

"I don't know. I'm not really feeling up to it right now."

"I was thinking tomorrow? I'd be happy to come pick you up. We can try calling the doctor from his place too. If for some strange reason he's not answering your calls, maybe he'll pick up if we call from a different number."

"Okay." Michelle sighed. "Yeah. Tomorrow after work. Hell, maybe your friend'll help cheer *me* up a bit."

In a moment of blind frustration, Darren had called Dr. Rains the night before. Rains hadn't answered, however, and now Darren was glad for that. What had he been thinking, calling some guy he met in a parking lot? Was he really a doctor? Could he prove it? It didn't matter much now. Darren had come to his senses.

His phantom limb was still filled with pain and discomfort, but it was bearable for the moment.

Darren had shifted gears, and was thinking about ordering a pizza for dinner when there was a knock at the door. The sound puzzled Darren for a moment. Had he called the order in already? Was he going crazy?

He answered the door. Dr. Rains stood before him.

"Good evening, Mr. Legend," he said. The shoulders of his overcoat were wet. Darren hadn't noticed that it had started raining.

"How...how'd you know my name?" Darren asked, suspicious.

"Oh, the support group. I went into the meeting

after running into you in the parking lot."

"Really?"

"Mr. Legend, please," Rains said. "I know what you're dealing with. Why, just the other day I helped a young woman whose legs were both amputated in a bizarre accident. She'd been experiencing such pain for years. But no longer. As I mentioned the other night, I've developed a procedure—"

"Well, thanks for stopping by, but I was just about to get some dinner." He tried closing the door, but Rains stopped it with a foot.

"Now, now, Darren," he said. "You need my help. And I need something from you." The doctor raised a hand to his mouth and blew. A puff of yellow powder exploded into Darren's face. His eyes rolled backward instantly, and his tongue fell out past his lips as he fell in a heap just inside the doorway.

"It really is so much easier when they just say yes," the doctor muttered to himself.

Rains stepped into the apartment, and dragged Darren's limp body in a few feet, just enough to get clearance with the door. He disappeared outside again for a moment, then returned, and rolled his trusty hand truck in.

The next day, Trina arrived at Darren's. She was about to knock on his door when she realized it wasn't completely latched. She pressed it lightly and it fell open.

"Darren?" she called out. "You here, hon?"

He didn't answer, but she found him sitting on the couch, eyes only half open.

"Hey. Darren. Did you know your door was open?" Trina paused. "Are you okay?" Then she said his name again, this time with more force.

"Yeah," he said, finally responding. "I'm...okay. I guess. My head is killing me."

"What happened? You look like hell."

Darren groaned. He got up and staggered to the bathroom, pulled a bottle from the medicine cabinet, and dry-swallowed a couple pills.

"You remembered I was coming over today, right?" Trina asked.

Darren nodded, his eyes closed, as he made his way back to the couch.

"I brought a friend over. Okay if she comes in?" Darren nodded again after falling back into the cushions. He looked up as Michelle rolled her chair through the doorway, and perked up.

"Whoa," he said, standing up, offering his left hand. "Michelle Mayfair! Of course! Wow, I watched you all summer long back when—"

"Hi Darren," Michelle said, shaking his hand. "Nice to meet you. Phantom limb's a bitch, right?"

Darren chuckled.

"So you remember that kook we met in the parking lot the other night?" Trina said. "Well, Michelle here knows a little bit about that 'procedure' he was going on about."

"Yeah, he quote-unquote *cured* me, so to speak," Michelle said. "Which is great. But something hasn't been quite right since I last saw him."

"He showed up here last night," Darren said.

"He *what*?!" said Trina.

"I don't know how he found me, but he just showed up and knocked on that door right there. I told him to take a hike, but he insisted on telling me about this procedure of his. Next thing I knew, I was trying to close the door, and I must have blacked out. I just woke up on the couch a few minutes ago."

"Did he have his hand truck with him?" asked Michelle.

"Hand truck? I don't remember. I don't remember much, actually. Just what I said. Why?"

"That procedure of his, it's really just a bunch of science gear on a hand truck," Michelle said. "Calls it the Phantom Zapper, if you can believe that shit."

"Come to think of it," Darren said, "as much as my head hurts, I can't feel my arm at all. I just noticed. And it's been bad lately."

"Okay, this is getting weird," said Trina. "What the heck happened? You think he knocked you out and cured you, and then bolted?"

"Yeah, well, I actually said yes to the procedure," said Michelle, "and I haven't heard from him since. I keep trying to call him, but he never answers."

"This guy's shady," said Trina.

"Yeah, I know. Something definitely feels, I don't know, *off*," said Darren.

"We need to track this guy down and get some answers," Trina said. "Do you still have his card, Darren?"

"I think it's on the table there. Maybe under my phone?"

"Got it," said Trina. "Just a name and number. Did you ever visit his office, Michelle?"

"Nope. It was all house calls. If he has an office, I have no idea where it is."

"We've got to find this quack," said Trina. "I mean, either he's rolling the invention of the century around on a hand truck, or he's up to no good. And since he seems to be dodging you, I'm betting on the latter."

Darren started to remember flashes of the night before. He remembered seeing a cloud of yellow dust, and falling, the back of his head slamming against the floor. He remembered the sound of a dinging bell, and something reminiscent of a full arm cast. He remembered seeing a pair of tires in the doorway, attached to something red, exiting the apartment.

"Lemme borrow your phone," said Michelle. "I know some people who might be able to help."

"You know some people?" said Darren.

"Well, I know some people who know some people…uh, who know some people. At least, I used to," she continued. "I don't know why I didn't think of this 'til now. I made a lot of contacts back in the day. I met a lot of politicians, and, well, one of them just might owe me a favor." She reached out her hand, beckoning the phone.

Trina prepared a warm washcloth and rested it on Darren's forehead while Michelle dialed dozens of digits into the phone, then uttered another series of numbers with her voice. A few more minutes passed in silence, then she began speaking in what seemed to be code words and vague phrases.

"Comma zero, alpha honeydew, monkey flank steak." Another pause. "Lipstick gas tank, maple town."

Trina was suddenly struck with a flood of ideas for new ice cream flavors. She started typing them into her phone. Apparently meeting with Michelle had quite suddenly paid off in the way her employer had intended.

"Empty lockout, flip cheese ladder, squeamish."

Darren just stared at Michelle from under the warm compress, trying to comprehend what was going on. Michelle paused again, and pivoted her chair, turning her back on him and Trina.

"Dirty grass, grape leaf quadrant. Rains, Griffin, possible alias."

"What is going on?" Trina whispered through her teeth to Darren, trying not to move her lips.

"Okay, thanks," Michelle said into the phone. Then

she ended the call and tossed the phone back to Darren. He was still a bit stunned, and didn't even reach out for the phone. It landed next to him, bouncing on the couch cushion.

"I got it," Michelle said. Darren's confused expression unscrewed slightly.

"You got it? Got what? An address?" Trina asked.

"Well, not quite yet. Like I said, I know some people. Granted, I haven't talked to some of these people in a couple years, but yeah."

"So, what exactly do you have?" asked Darren.

"I've got an appointment set up for tomorrow. Like I said, someone I did a favor for a long time ago knows someone who knows someone who knows someone. And one of those someones is going to call me back in the morning, hopefully with an address."

"Hopefully?" said Trina.

"Well, like I said, it's been a few years. But I saved this guy's marriage a long time ago, so hopefully he comes through. He should."

"Okay, so...should we touch base again tomorrow morning? Here?" Trina asked.

"Sure," said Michelle. "Pick me up again?"

Trina nodded. "What do you think, Darren? Breakfast?"

"I'll have pancakes ready," he said.

Dr. Rains had found the process of applying ConnECTO to his phantom limb collection to be considerably more difficult than he had expected. But he also found the challenge to be fun. It was like struggling with a cat in a bathtub—only he now had hundreds of these critters, and they were all able to pass through other objects, necessitating the use of electrical charges to wrangle them—charges that also caused the phantoms to grow slightly with each shock.

Having an extra pair of limbs, in this instance, was convenient. He simply used one rubber-gloved hand to administer a small shock, two others to hold each phantom down, and the last to apply the ConnECTO. The only real issue was that he didn't like the feel of the thick elbow-length gloves he had to wear in order to do the job. He preferred to feel the science directly with his hands.

Rigging the borders of the secondary lab space, the mostly empty room he was using to facilitate the assembly of his creation, with electric fencing material, had been a hassle. The contractor he hired to secure the room had to be disposed of as soon as the job was done, and Rains had not given him quite enough poison at first.

That had been a rough night, chasing the contractor through the streets at dusk, forcing more poison down his throat, waiting for his flesh to break apart and dissolve, then stretching a series of hoses down the street from the lab, so that he could wash the wet pile of remains into a sewer grate.

Finding four-armed lab coats had been difficult too, especially in the "Howie" style he preferred, with the side closure, shoulder buttons, and Mandarin collar, but that was something he had dealt with years prior.

Now he had a surplus of them stored in a closet, having bought a variety pack of a few hundred of them from a manufacturer in Japan. They came in a plethora of colors, none of them classic white. Some were solid colors, while others had ornate patterns. It didn't matter to Rains, though—he was used to standing out, being different. He rather liked the purple lab coat he had on now. It had an intricate but barely perceptible pattern of smiling cats woven into the vertical stripes.

His work was just about done. After several years of research, experiments, trial and error, his latest creation was almost completely assembled, and his revenge would be had soon enough. He began to salivate and shake with anticipation, but quickly calmed himself.

Rains took a break and stepped into the main laboratory. Sexy the Sexopus was there, and perked up when he entered the room, hoping it was time for a feeding. It wasn't.

The television mounted above Sexy's tank was on. The talking head on the screen mentioned that the *Science Now!* conference taking place downtown would begin the following morning. A small number of tickets would be made available to the public, but for the most part, this was an event meant for members of the scientific community. Rains wondered which camp he would fall into if the issue was put to a vote by those stooges.

He tossed the spent tube of ConnECTO he was holding in the direction of an overflowing trash can in the corner. Before letting go, he gave it one last squeeze, and imagined it to be the mangled corpse of one of his so-called "colleagues". *Detractors* was more like it. It landed on a pile of curled and wrinkled tubes, each of them recently emptied and squashed by Rains' fist. Each one reminded him of a different scientist he had encountered over the course of his career. They had all kept him outside the inner circle, kept him away from the fame and fortune he so rightly deserved. They all deserved to be gutted and cast aside. This was good practice. He hoped the remaining phantoms in the room were paying attention.

Dr. Griffin Rains finished his work late that night, and found himself exhausted from the hours spent wrangling hundreds of phantom limbs and applying ConnECTO to them. But tired as he was, he was also content. He removed his quartet of black rubber gloves, unbuttoned his coat at the shoulder, and wiped the beads of sweat from the top of his head with a sleeve. He took off his goggles and moved to his makeshift bedroom, which was essentially a large closet with a mattress on the floor. He left the TV on in the main lab for background noise, and to keep Sexy the Sexopus company. *Godzilla vs. The Smog Monster* was on.

Although he was content, there was excitement welling inside him too, which negated the possibility of much sleep. He did manage to fall unconscious for an hour or two, but that was it. During that time, he dreamt of monsters—vile, horrid beasts with black tongues and razor claws, who seemed hell-bent on destroying everything in their path—except for Rains. When they reached him, they attacked him in a fit of celebration, lifting him up onto their scaly shoulders and passing him around. Suddenly there were party hats and streamers, confetti and cake. A grand, colorful party erupted in the middle of the gray chaos, and Dr. Rains was the guest of honor.

Upon waking, the doctor was still smiling. The dream was nonsense, of course, but had served as a sort of pep rally for the big unveiling that would be taking place the following evening.

Science Now?, the doctor thought. *Soon enough.*

"Pancakes are ready. Where are you guys?" Darren said into the phone. He had Trina on speaker, so he was able to pour the last bit of batter on the griddle.

"The plan changed a bit," Trina said. "I'm over at her place now. She's been on the phone for a while. I have no idea what she's been saying, but it sounds like we need to wait until tonight."

"Tonight? Why?"

"Cover of darkness. Apparently we need to break into the place." Trina said.

"Break in?" said Darren. "I don't know about this. This is...This is turning into something a little bigger than I had anticipated."

"How's your arm, Darren?" Michelle was speaking to him now, having grabbed Trina's phone after ending her other call abruptly.

"It's...not—" Darren said. "I mean, I don't feel the phantom limb anymore."

"The rest of you doesn't feel quite right either, does

it?" Michelle said.

Darren hesitated a moment before answering. "No," he said. "I don't know how to explain it. I just don't feel... *complete*. And not in the obvious, literal way."

"And it's a little worse today than it was last night, isn't it?" Michelle said.

"How'd you know?" Darren asked, surprised.

"I'm going through the same thing as you, buddy. But I'm a few days ahead. And let me tell you, it's just gonna get worse, then worse. It's kinda fucked up, but honestly, the only thing keeping me going at this point is that I want this doctor to pay for what he's done. Whatever it is that he's done. Otherwise, I'd probably be a wreck right now."

Darren didn't respond.

Trina yelled from the background. "We've got to find this guy and figure out what's going on, Darren. What he did to you both. We need some answers."

"And we've got to break into Rains' office to do that?" Darren asked.

"Well, he's not exactly the most honest guy in the world," Michelle said. "My contact says they've actually been keeping an eye on Rains for a while now. They knew he was shady, but didn't know exactly what he was up to."

Darren could hear Trina in the background again. "Who's this contact of yours? What do you mean 'they'?"

"He may have a lot to hide in that office of his," Michelle continued. "And if he sees us strolling up to it—the office he doesn't seem to want anyone knowing about—well, that's not gonna go well. My guy seems to think we'll get more answers if we stop in while the doc is out."

"*This* seems a little shady," Darren said.

"I know," said Michelle. "We'll pick you up after dark."

Shortly after the sun disappeared, Trina and Michelle picked up Darren. The three of them drove into the Warehouse District, and passed by the address Michelle's contact had given them. Trina made sure not to slow down in front of it, just in case anyone happened to be looking. It wasn't the greatest part of town, but plenty of people lived there, in condos and loft spaces that seemed to pop up out of nowhere, interspersed here and there among the myriad abandoned factories and warehouses.

"Definitely doesn't look like a doctor's office," Darren said.

They parked a few blocks away and split up, each taking a different route through the surrounding blocks. Trina and Darren met up a few minutes later in front of the address. The building, some sort of modified warehouse, was poorly lit. There were windows in front, but no doors. Oddly enough, there was a wheelchair ramp that ran directly into a cinder block wall.

"The entrance is back here," whispered Michelle,

rolling around the corner, motioning backward with her head.

A few minutes later, Michelle was putting an old skill to use—picking the lock on the door in near-record time.

"Running more than likely kept me out of prison," she said with a shrug. The door eased open and the three of them moved in as quietly as they could.

The interior was lit by a handful of fluorescent lights scattered irregularly throughout the space, leaving plenty of dim spaces and dark corners.

There were several small rooms near the entrance, and each of them seemed to be largely for storage. One was filled with nothing but an assortment of very colorful coats, some on hangers, but many just piled in cardboard boxes. The smallest room held nothing but a dirty mattress. Another contained a series of connected fish tanks. The aquariums were filled with water, somewhat murky, each tinted a dingy brown. There were body parts inside—some human, some covered with scales and suckers. Some of them floated and moved, others lay lifeless at the bottoms of their tanks.

A silver tray sat on a small corner table, containing what appeared to be a larger-than-average chicken heart. Clear tubes ran in and out of it, while red fluid pulsed through them. The heart was beating.

"What the fuck?" said Michelle, keeping her voice low. Darren and Trina were startled as much by the voice as the sights in front of them, but they both remained quiet.

At the end of the main hall, the space expanded into a larger room—Dr. Griffin Rains' main laboratory. They moved in, exploring the space, which was illuminated mainly by the dim glow of a hundred or so small machines, each with a different arrangement of LEDs and electronic displays.

There were tables everywhere, covered with glassware—beakers, test tubes, globes with roller coaster piping twisted all about, mysterious liquids, heating elements. The walls were lined with shelves and glass cases all the way up to the ceiling, some covered with drop cloths, others bare and empty. Plastic tubing seemed to come from every direction, curling in and around dozens of active experiments. There was so much going on, it was tough to tell what the doctor was focused on, but it was clear there was something more to him than his career as a phantom limb therapist.

"What the hell is this guy up to?" asked Darren, sure to keep his voice low, now that he was talking. Something in the corner caught his eye—a giant octopus, of all things, floating inside an aquarium. An octopus with six tentacles and two stumps.

"Whoa. If this guy could talk..." Trina said, noticing the octopus. She stepped toward the creature, and locked eyes with him. "I think he's asking for help," she said.

She took another step toward the creature and lost her footing. "What the—"

"What's wrong?" asked Darren, keeping quiet.

"I'm okay. I just slipped on some garbage," she whispered. "But it's weird garbage. A big pile of toothpaste tubes or something." Trina kicked a stray tube back into the pile. "Wait a
second."

Trina picked up one of the spent tubes, and flattened it out. The label on the face read "ConnECTO". She flipped it over.

"Hmm... 'Recommended for wood, porcelain, vinyl, stone, canvas/fabrics, floor tiles, fiberglass...and ghosts?' This is some kind of adhesive?"

"What? A friggin' glue for ghosts? Holy shit!" Michelle said.

"Yeah, and he made packaging for it?" asked Darren. "Like, with a label and everything? What ego!"

Michelle rolled her way over to Trina, bumping a table on the way. A beaker hit the floor and shattered. Everyone froze.

A dull thump sounded from one of the rooms down the hall. A moment of silence was followed by another thump, then a crash, like metal clanging on ceramic tile.

Dr. Rains stood, anxiously, just off-stage at the *Science Now!* convention, camouflaged by the curtains. He had worn his custom black Howie lab coat this evening, the one with the Japanese demon mask—a Hannya—embroidered on the back, to help blend into the darkness. He was shaking, but it was more excitement than nervousness. He couldn't wait to reveal his presence, and that of his greatest creation yet, to the unsuspecting crowd of his so-called scientific peers. He adjusted the strap on his goggles, and scratched his temple.

From the wings, he watched the keynote speaker deliver his address, but didn't hear a word of it. He was boiling inside, the anticipation bubbling in his ears. To calm himself, he thought about how clever he had been, hiring migrant workers to help him transport his creation to the convention center. He made sure they didn't speak English, and he gave them each a case of beer in addition to some counterfeit cash as payment.

The beer was his own special brew too, composed

mostly of an odorless, tasteless poison—something he had used before. He wondered if the workers even made it home before cracking into their reward. It didn't matter. Either way, they were just puddles of their former selves by now.

"Excuse me, sir," said a stagehand, appearing beside Rains as if from nowhere, "but we're going to have to ask you to take your seat." He was dressed completely in black, just as Rains was.

Rains was startled, having been lost in his thoughts. He made a sound, but hadn't been quick enough to offer an excuse. He just stared at the stagehand.

"Sir? We need to clear this space now, to make way for the award presentation."

Rains looked the stagehand in the eye, and tensed his own brow. "Do you know who I am?" he said, as he reached into his pocket.

"Sir, virtually everyone here is a VIP," said the stagehand. "But everyone who's not part of this award presentation needs to take their seat right now."

"You don't know who I am, do you?" the doctor said, pulling his hand from his pocket, and raising it up to his own face. He took a deep breath and blew into the powder he was holding. A cloud of yellow smoke exploded into the stagehand's face, and he dropped to the ground immediately. "You'll know my name soon enough," Rains said. Then he turned his attention back to the speaker on the stage.

Michelle, Darren, and Trina had a quick conversation with their eyes: *Someone's here. Should we go? We gotta get outta here! What the fuck are we waiting around for?!* But before they could act, something entered the room from the far corner. Two things, in fact, each semi-transparent, and glowing green from within.

"Oh shit," said Michelle. "The guard dogs are here."

The first of them looked like a mutant starfish—three human legs and two arms, all a bit larger than they should have been, all attached at a central point. Despite its monstrous appearance, however, it spun into the room cautiously, in a slow cartwheel roll.

The second thing followed closely behind. It was a pair of larger-than-average human legs, connected by what looked like a forearm across the top, like a ghostly, mobile Stonehenge with a floppy hand hanging over the top of one leg. It walked in like any normal pair of legs might, if legs could walk without a body. It took short strides, perhaps unsure of its movements.

Trina screamed. There was no point in being quiet any longer. Even the octopus in the tank had suddenly become more animated, undulating his arms, occasionally splashing water over the top edge of the case.

"Whoa...Are those...are those phantom limbs?" Darren asked.

"Fuck! That's it!" said Michelle, stunned. She had her hands on her wheels, but didn't move.

"What's it?" said Trina.

"That's what that body cast contraption was all about. It wasn't a pain-relief procedure. That bastard was actually stealing our phantom limbs."

"Wait, what? What body cast thing?" asked Trina.

The mutant pair lit up the dark corner of the room, their green aura reflecting off the shelves and the glassware on the tables. They sounded like static, buzzing softly. Every few seconds, they would burst with flashes from within. Lightning struck inside their forms, erratically, like sparks of anger, explosions of light and energy. They moved forward slowly, cautiously.

"Rains' procedure," said Michelle. "That science gear I was telling you about? It's a sort of machine he uses, all attached to a hand truck. Looks like a body cast, with detachable sections. He separated the legs from the contraption, and told me to slide my phantom legs into them. Next thing I knew, I couldn't feel them anymore."

"What does that even mean?" asked Trina.

"No, it makes sense, doesn't it?" said Darren. "You know, like *Ghostbusters*. They had that box they rolled out into the middle of a room, and they sucked the ghosts right up."

"Yeah, like a friggin' ghost vacuum!" said Michelle. "Like, my legs are gone, but for a while, the ghosts of my legs remained. Until he stole them away from me. Same with your arm, Darren."

"So what now? What's the point?" asked Trina. Then she answered her own question. "ConnECTO. Whoa."

"Yup. Franken-ghosts," said Michelle, quieter now, hoping not to startle the abominations creeping toward them. "Freak doctor's actually a mad scientist."

Stonehenge and the Starfish continued moving forward tentatively. They were translucent and gaseous, able to pass through objects with ease. Until they sparked from within. Each crash of electricity seemed to make them not only fully visible, but solid. In this state, they could touch and move objects.

The Starfish rolled forward and lit up just as it was about to pass through a table. Its form solidified, and it crashed into the table instead, scattering several racks of test tubes, which fell to the tile floor below and shattered.

"These things are a mess," said Darren. "They must be experiments. Like test runs."

"Yeah. They don't have eyes, so they must not be able to see us," said Trina. "But they do seem to know we're here. And I don't think they're too happy about it."

"Well whatever they are, they're pretty fucked up," said Michelle. "I'm gonna say it's time for us to leave."

Trina pulled her phone out, thinking quickly to take a picture of the two monstrosities. Proof would more than likely come in handy later; surely no one would believe the story. But as soon as she had the phone in hand, the screen flickered and flipped. The hum of static in the room rose suddenly, and she actually felt the phone sizzle, shaking in her hand. A puff of white smoke jumped from the corner of the device as it died in her palm.

Stonehenge dashed forward toward Trina, but lit up and crashed into a glass case. The ghost-legs fell to the floor, somersaulted, then stood back up. It was like a newborn calf, anxious but unsure of its movements, stumbling down and getting back up.

The octopus became more agitated in his aquarium, splashing water over the top of the tank, momentarily distracting the ghosts.

"Go!" Trina grabbed the handles of Michelle's wheelchair and pushed, navigating their way around the tables and broken glass. Darren followed behind them, running backwards to keep an eye on the monsters.

"And, while keeping his many accomplishments in mind, it's also worth pointing out that he's a rather wonderful man..." The presenter smiled wide with perfect pearlescent teeth, one hand on the podium, the other cradling a golden statuette as he spoke into the microphone.

"Ladies and gentlemen, it is my pleasure and distinct honor to introduce the recipient of this year's *Scientist of the Last 365 and a Quarter Days Award*—"

"Just a moment, sir!" The voice came from off-stage. It echoed through the grand ballroom, un-amplified. There was a commotion in the wings, stage-left. Dr. Rains was fighting his way onto the stage, through several stagehands who seemed to want to stop him, but simultaneously didn't want to make too much of a scene. "Just a moment!"

Dr. Rains approached the podium, and smiled at the presenter before snatching the statuette from his hands and hip-checking him out of the way.

"Ladies and gentlemen," he announced. "My apologies for the intrusion, but we have a bit of a special attraction to share with you before handing out this award." He set the gold trophy on the floor, on its side, showing it no reverence.

"Many of you know me. For those of you who don't, I'm certain you've heard my name whispered among your colleagues. I would like to think my name is spoken with an air of respect, perhaps some degree of jealousy. But over the years, I've learned it is simply spoken with the same weight as that of your weekly garbage men, or perhaps the pimple-faced boy who bags your groceries.

"If there is any doubt as to my identity—I realize some of you are sitting rather far away—My name is Dr. Griffin Rains."

The crowd tittered. Several scientists and their scientist-spouses gasped.

"Yes, *that* Dr. Rains. You know me. I am the one behind the Aluminum Siding Tree, the one who built the Helium Swingset. And now, as of tonight, I shall be known as the inventor of the world's first paranormal adhesive, ConnECTO—*patent pending, by the way*—and by extension, the father of this magnificent beast here!"

Something gigantic rolled out from behind the rear curtains. It was draped in an enormous patchwork cloth, which appeared to have been stitched together from dingy curtains, bedsheets and drop cloths. The thing underneath it stood fifty feet tall, and bumped the lighting rigs above the stage.

Dr. Rains paused his speech, and glanced back at the giant cloak. His lips curled.

"May we have a spotlight please?" he asked. The person in charge of the spotlight did not comply.

"Oh well. No matter." He walked over to the hidden thing, and with one swift tug, removed the drapes, revealing a magnificent monster. "May I present to you my latest creation: *the SuperGhost!*"

It was a tower of translucent body parts, all glowing green. It stood on two gigantic legs, each the sum of several dozen larger-than-average phantom legs, all attached end-to-end and woven together like braided hair, to form a pair of ghostly redwood-sized trunks on which to stand. Not that the thing needed to stand. It was a ghost. It could float, perhaps fly, just as easily as it could walk.

Perched atop the legs was a single massive, muscular translucent green torso—like that of a bodybuilder—with a single head, and a dozen arms. The arms were nearly as big as the legs, each woven together the same way, each the product of who knows how many people. There were even a pair of tentacles coming out of the neck, like a weird, sucker-lined, living bolo tie.

The monster glowed green with the aura of a radioactive lime. It buzzed and sizzled, electricity rolling through it, as if each limb was a Jacob's Ladder. It was a ghostly King Kong, but much stranger.

Waves of panic shot through the audience. A hundred gasps led to a hundred outright screams. Some jumped up from their seats and raced toward the exits, while others were too scared to move.

"What is that?" they said. "What have you done?" they screamed. "Why, oh why?" they shrieked.

"To show you!" Rains shouted above the chaos, ignoring the microphone that stood to his right. "To show you it could be done. To show you I am not worthy of your derision, or your pity. To show you that I am indeed a *Scientist* with a capital S, and that my so-called crazy ideas aren't so crazy after all, and that they might just lead to something big someday. Well, my 'friends'—*that day is now!*

"I wouldn't bother running for the doors, by the way. They've all been secured from the outside. There's no getting out of here. There's no escape. No escape from *judgment!*

"That's right. It's time for you all to be judged, just as you've judged me!" He raised his fists in the air. "You want science? Well here it is! *Science Now! Hahahaha!*"

Back in the car, dashing away from the Warehouse District, Trina turned on the radio. A frantic reporter, out of breath, delivered the details.

"Eyewitness reports are still trickling in, with many saying that a noted scientist—one who was often shunned by his peers—stormed the stage tonight during a presentation at the *Science Now!* convention. Some say the scientist, named by several attendees as a Dr. Griffin Rains, hijacked the proceedings and unleashed some sort of monster on the audience. *Is that right? A monster?* Yes, we're getting reports of a creature, some *fifty feet tall*, with literally *dozens* of arms and legs, attacking several conference attendees and destroying a section of the grand ballroom before crashing through a glass wall and escaping into the city. Witnesses are saying the monster has a pale green complexion, and is...*see-through?* Is that right? Yes, see-through.

"98-X News is encouraging individuals in the downtown area to leave their homes, unless their homes happen to be reinforced underground bunkers.

"We must note at this time that 98-X News has so far been unable to independently verify the identity of the so-called terrorist as Dr. Rains, but we are working to do so as we speak."

"Well, that's one question answered," said Trina. "Now what?"

"Now we go downtown," said Michelle.

"What?" said Trina.

"She's right," said Darren. "We may be the only ones who have any clue at all what's going on. We've got to find a reporter, or tell the police, or something."

"Fine. How do we get to the convention center?" Trina asked.

"See that cloud of smoke?" Michelle said. "Head for that."

Getting to the source of the smoke wasn't easy. Traffic was backed up, and people were running through the streets, all trying to run away from the chaos, while Trina was attempting to drive toward it.

Eventually they got close. They came upon the near side of the convention center, now a pile of rubble spilled out into the street. Chunks of stone, broken glass, and twisted rebar lay everywhere. There were bodies, too.

From where they were forced to stop, the debris seemed to form a path several blocks long, like a misplaced jetty bordered by lacerated buildings, from the convention center all the way down the road to the main library, at least.

"We need to go there," said Darren as he unloaded Michelle's wheelchair from the hatchback. "We've got to do what we can."

"You guys go ahead," said Michelle. "I won't be able to make it through the rubble."

Without saying a word, Trina nodded at Michelle,

then grabbed Darren's hand and started moving.

Terrified voices shrieked as they ran past Darren and Trina. "It's a monster!" some screamed. "Ghost!" others yelled. Darren and Trina glanced at each other and pressed on.

After ten minutes of moving as quickly as possible through heaps of concrete and twisted steel, they finally found themselves in front of the library. The street lamps on the sidewalk outside it were still standing, but they flickered, while the traffic lights lying in the middle of the intersection were flashing all three colors at once. Cars lay on their sides, crumpled like balls of tin foil.

Darren and Trina stopped moving toward the building when they heard a deep rumble from inside it, like the worst case of indigestion ever recorded. Then something crashed within, and puffs of smoke escaped from the doorways. A second floor window burst, and a dozen books flew out and fluttered to the ground like dying birds. A handful of people escaped through doorways and windows, wide-eyed and manic.

A corner of the building exploded. An avalanche of concrete rolled into the street as tiny bits of glass rained down on Darren. Trina had been fast enough to dive and find shelter behind a group of newspaper boxes.

A minute later, after hearing the dust settle, Darren cracked open his eyes and scanned the area for Trina.

"Right here!" she announced, raising a hand above the top edge of the metal newspaper boxes, now dented and covered in gray dust. "You okay?"

"Yeah." Darren pulled a chunk of glass from the corner of his eye. Luckily it hadn't penetrated. It simply stuck there, flat against the skin. "That was close," he said, flicking it to the ground. Millimeters to the left would have meant blindness.

Trina's lips parted. She pointed past Darren, in the direction of the library, as she rose slowly from her knees. He spun around to see what she was seeing. Through a hole in the corner of the now-ruined building, they could see flickering light glowing from within.

Green light.

Then, seconds later, as more dust cleared, the giant ghostly beast emerged. Darren and Trina quietly said "uh-oh" in unison.

The thing stood nearly sixty feet tall now, having grown even more since crashing out of the convention center and traveling down the street. It was a grotesque tower of translucent limbs, filled with lightning. There were dozens of arms and legs, limbs extending from other limbs, all sprouting like gnarled tree branches from one central point. At the middle of it all was the ghostly torso and head of a strongman. That part, at least, still appeared somewhat human, but its voice made an unearthly sound when the monster stepped out of the building completely, roaring into the air.

"Well," Trina said, "I guess we don't technically need to tell anyone about the freaky ghost-things we saw in the lab."

The creature took a monstrous step toward the pair.

In the background, people were still screaming. A helicopter passed overhead. Sirens shrieked in the distance. A fire raged just a block away.

Rising above the sounds of terror, however, was a

single voice that Darren recognized. It was Dr. Rains, and he was laughing.

"Oh, hello, Mr. Legend! Behold the SuperGhost!" he said. Darren turned to see the mad scientist standing atop a pile of concrete ruins that had surrounded the post of a stop sign. A tattered American flag, presumably one that had fallen from one of the buildings above, was draped over his shoulders. "What do you think?"

Darren found himself unable to respond immediately.

"It's quite a marvel, wouldn't you say?" the doctor continued. "I spent a lot of time—not to mention considerable funds—putting this guy together. The least you can do is share your impressions with me.

"Of course, I suppose a thank you is in order first, considering your contribution to the cause. So three cheers to you, Mr. Legend. *Hurrah! Hurrah! Hurrah!*"

Darren looked at the beast, and instantly spotted his own phantom limb in a tangle of arms on the creature's right side.

"What are you doing?" yelled Trina.

"Oh hello, dear. And who might you be?" asked Rains, rather calmly.

"We met in the parking lot. What do you want?" she responded.

"Want? Why, whatever I want, I'll simply take!" Rains gestured toward the glowing monster. "And this fellow here, my greatest creation yet, will be the means."

"That doesn't exactly answer her question, does it?" asked Darren. "I mean, what are you doing? What's the point of all this, Rains? It's madness!"

The doctor chuckled, kicking a chunk of jagged concrete off his perch.

"Sometimes bold gestures are necessary, my friend. I am a man of Science. *That's Science with a capital S, mind you.* I have ideas. Grand ideas. World-changing ideas. But people aren't always ready—or willing—to listen. Sometimes they would rather make fun of you, berate you, or marginalize your impact. It may be based on something childish, such as one's appearance, or one's demeanor, or it may be based in simple jealousy. But no matter the reason for the derision of my peers in the scientific community, I know that my ideas are important ones. I know that *they*, and that *I*, matter. So I had to get a leg up, so to speak. I had to do something to *make those deaf ears listen.*"

"You're crazy!" yelled Darren.

"Are you not thankful, Mr. Legend? Not only were you able to contribute to one of the most spectacular scientific breakthroughs in the history of the world, but you no longer have those nagging pains where your arm once was. No more discomfort. I assume you've been sleeping through the night lately. Are you not happier now?"

"Actually, no," said Darren. "When I woke up after you knocked me out, I knew something wasn't right. Now I can see what. I may not have been able to feel the sensation of my phantom limb any more, but my body must have known, somehow, where my phantom had gone, and what it was being used for. Like my body had some sort of psychic link to the missing part."

"Ha! *The missing link!* I wish I had come up with that one. Anyway, that's very interesting. You know, you're not too far off with your assumption. After all, that's how I'm able to control this behemoth right here."

"Meaning?" asked Darren.

Dr. Rains raised his front arms, dropping the flag from his shoulders, revealing a third arm. Trina's jaw dropped. Darren was surprised, but his expression didn't change. It wasn't the strangest thing he'd seen all day.

"Meaning," the doctor said, "that in order to launch my creation upon the eyes and ears of the world, I had to take matters into my own hands." Rains gestured across his body with his third arm, and pointed to the limp fourth sleeve of his black lab coat. "I had to create my very own phantom limb."

"Oh man," said Trina, under her breath.

"Then I had to harvest it, and attach it to my friend the SuperGhost here. See that hand up there? The one brandishing an angry fist? That's me.

"And that psychic link you spoke of? Well, that's not far off. Since a part of me is attached to the great beast, I'm able to control it."

"So by that logic, I should be able to take him down," Darren said.

"Not quite. That's only part of it, I'm afraid. There is the physical-psychic link, of course, which you and I both have in this case. But I have a mental-psychic link too. That bodybuilder you see in the center of it all? That's my brother. My *twin* brother."

The phantom torso flexed, as if it was on stage at a competition.

"You see, all our lives, he was the popular one. He had the body, and that body brought the ladies. The ladies gave him the confidence, and that confidence gave him everything else. I was the scrawny mutant freak. But at least I had the brains.

"Years ago, my dear brother had an unfortunate accident, in which he lost a leg. And that's when this all began. When opportunities present themselves, one must act quickly. Before long, I had devised a series of experiments. I found a way to remove phantom limbs. Then, by electrical means, I found a way to capture and control them. And my brother here donated the rest of his being—in ghost form, that is.

"All that remained from there was devising a way to make the phantoms grow a bit bigger—Electricity's still a marvel, wouldn't you say?—And then to combine and connect them all into a single SuperGhost. Now here we are."

"Yeah, we know about your ghost glue," said Trina.

"ConnECTO! Great name, right?"

"We went to your lab," said Trina. "We know there are others." She paused. "What are you doing? Building an army?"

"Ah, but this one's *arm-y* enough, wouldn't you say? This guy's got at least two dozen arms right here." Dr. Rains laughed. He seemed unconcerned about the break-in at the lab. "In all seriousness, however, those were mere sketches. They'll expire soon enough. They probably won't even make it outside, unless you left the door open. You didn't leave the door open, did you?

"Oh well. No matter. As I said, they'll die off before too long. At least, I think they will. In any event, I must say they were quite useful experiments. I learned a lot from them."

"So now you've made your big statement, right?"

said Trina, attempting to reason with the mad doctor. "At the expense of life, and limb. Not to mention the property damage. We get it. Let's shut it down and go home."

"Oh, I don't know about that. Surely there's a bit more to accomplish, having gone this far. Right? How would you like to join me? Come on—I'd be happy to make you a part of—"

A single gunshot pierced the scene. Dr. Rains stood perfectly still for a moment at the top of the concrete pile, trapped forever in mid-sentence by the hole in his forehead and the red line that dribbled from it. Then he dropped dead in a heap.

"No!" Trina was manic. "We could have...we could have *reasoned* with him!"

Darren stood beside her, wide-eyed in shock.

Across the street, standing atop another pile of broken building pieces, was a lone police officer. He looked young. His legs were shaking. Six other cops jumped on him, and wrestled the gun from his hands.

Darren and Trina were shaking too, unsure of what to do, or where to run. Rains was suddenly gone, and the monster he had created didn't appear to be ready for any sort of negotiation.

The SuperGhost growled, angry and panicked, and raised a dozen fists into the air, shaking them violently. A surge of electricity exploded inside it, lighting up what was left of the intersection. Darren and Trina could see that they, and the SuperGhost, were now surrounded by at least a hundred armed police officers. The SuperGhost roared again, a declaration of supremacy tinged with fear and anger. It stomped on a pile of broken concrete, and turned it into gravel, then returned back toward the library and punched the side of it, pulverizing the brick face instantly. Another lightning strike crashed inside the SuperGhost as the beast tore a lamppost out of the sidewalk like a weed, and tossed it at the ring of police officers closing in.

"We're not a part of this!" screamed Trina, waving her hands back and forth, terrified. Darren wrapped his arm around her and pulled her down to take cover. Especially now that Rains was dead, the SuperGhost was looking more and more unpredictable as the seconds ticked by.

"Now! Launch 'em!" yelled one of the officers. And with that, two giant nets, each weighted around their perimeters with lead spheres, were shot from cannons on opposite sides of the street. They expanded like flying squirrels in mid-air, arcing toward the SuperGhost. But just before landing, the SuperGhost's light went out, and the nets passed right through the translucent monster, falling limply to the ground.

Another shock of lightning lit the beast up from within. It growled again, and shot sparks from a couple hundred fingertips. Several cops found themselves in the path of the lightning, and were shocked where they stood. The air around them sizzled. It wasn't quite enough to electrocute them, but it did make their hair stand up.

"Foam!" yelled the officer in charge. Ten cops fired from massive rubber hoses. Thick pink suds shot forth, like cotton candy fountains. The monster jumped upward, and hovered, floating above the foam as it collected on the ground beneath it.

"Motherfucker!" yelled one officer. Frustrated, he

threw a handful of gravel in the direction of the monster, but didn't come close to reaching it.

"It's a ghost, duh," muttered Trina with an incredulous look on her face. "Of course it can float."

"There's nothing we can do here," Darren said, trying to stay as clear-headed as possible. "We need to go. Now."

"Okay. Where?"

A Humvee screeched around the corner, stopping just short of a concrete heap.

"Get in!" It was Michelle. They could hear the voice, but all they saw was a hand waving just past the top edge of a rock pile. "Come on! Hurry!"

Darren and Trina ran for it, jumping over shattered windows and twisted girders. "She drives?" asked Trina, as quiet as she could while running through what had turned into a warzone.

"Hey guys," said Michelle, hanging out the window of the Humvee, nearly as out-of-breath as Trina and Darren. She motioned toward the driver's seat. "This is Hank. Friend of a friend, of a friend, blah blah blah. Get in."

"Hi, Hank. Thanks," said Trina as they jumped into the back seat. Hank nodded from behind a pair of unnecessary sunglasses, and stepped on the gas. He had a knack for maneuvering around chaos.

"Yeah. Thanks, man," said Darren. "How'd you know where to find us?"

"We set the GPS for Big Green Ghost," said Michelle. "*You fucking serious?* We drove toward the destruction."

A minute later, they were already out of harm's way, and the SuperGhost was shrinking in the rear view mirror.

Thirty minutes later, they were holed up at Michelle's apartment.

Hank was in the bedroom, on the phone. The door

was closed, and he spoke in a hushed voice. Darren wasn't able to decipher a word, so he quickly stopped trying, and focused his attention on the TV instead. The news was on.

Without its master, the SuperGhost was like a hurricane with claws. It was moving, more or less, in a ragged spiral pattern from the center point of the city outward, wreaking havoc, destroying everything in its path. The monster punched holes in buildings, ripped utility poles out of the ground, and stomped on parked cars, flattening them like pancakes. Gray dust blanketed everything. There were trails of blood now too. The SuperGhost had started picking up sheets of metal and still somehow-unbroken glass, and tossing them like Frisbees in the direction of anyone it encountered. Half the police force had already suffered casualties. Scientists had been decapitated. The death toll was growing, with the bodies of bystanders littering the streets.

And the SuperGhost's size and power both seemed to only be expanding. At one intersection, it shot lightning from a hundred fingertips once again. This time, however, those it hit were electrocuted. Bodies fried instantly and fell, smoking and crispy.

"Crazy as it is to say this," Trina said, "that thing is kind of amazing. Just like the smaller ones in the lab, it's able to transition from nearly-transparent nothingness into a physical being. I mean, it can pass through things when it wants, and it can tear into things when it wants. Just look at that!"

The footage being broadcast from the helicopter over the scene showed the monster pass through traffic lights, then pick up cars, and toss them aside. It passed through one building, then knocked into the next.

"Incredible," Trina said. "Horrible."

Then the news footage showed something else. The SuperGhost was filling itself with power, becoming solid, then grabbing whichever humans were in reach. Lifting bodies into the air with any one of its hands, the beast then tore off limbs, like a child pulling legs from spiders.

Casting the severed limbs aside, the beast held onto its prey for as long as necessary. Before long, a phantom—the ghost of each limb—would appear, and the SuperGhost would fuse itself to it. In just a matter of hours, the SuperGhost had found a way to grow even larger, and add even more appendages to its mass. It was a terrifying prospect.

"This is..." said Darren. "This is... We've got to do something."

"Easier said than done," said Trina.

"Maybe. But I'm a part of that thing. And on top of that, it's destroying my city. I helped build half of those buildings. And now I'm partially responsible for all this chaos..."

"Well, let's not get carried away. You may be part of it, in a way. But it was completely unwilling. And beyond your control."

"No, he's right," interrupted Michelle. "I'm feeling the same way. That thing has my legs. My phantom legs, at least."

"Okay, so what are you suggesting?" asked Trina.

"Well, it just so happens that while you two were in the middle of your standoff with Rains, Hank came by to pick me up. How he knew I was down there, I don't know, but he picked me up about thirty seconds after we all parted ways. Anyway, he knows my contact somehow—the one who gave us Rains' address. So he picked me up, I filled him in on what we found in the lab, and apparently now his guys are working on something. Granted, it's a little kooky, but it just might work."

"Uhh..." said Trina.

"Surely it's no kookier than the idea of a giant ghost monster made from phantom limbs," said Darren.

"I guess you could say it's about the same level of kookiness," said Michelle.

Michelle, Trina, and Darren all had their eyes glued to the television. The news was getting even worse. They didn't even realize Hank had hung up his phone and come out of the bedroom.

"Okay, Michelle. My guys are ready," he said.

Darren and Trina both looked at Michelle, then looked at each other, confused.

"Hank, why don't you go grab a smoke while I fill these folks in a bit?" She paused while Hank left the apartment and waited on the sidewalk.

"So, it turns out my friends-of-friends-of-friends were keeping an eye on things all along. As in, before I had any idea myself. Before Rains ever set foot through my door. Turns out he had been stealing these phantom limbs for a few years. This SuperGhost of his was a long time in the making. My friends just hadn't put all the pieces together, so to speak, until...well, until downtown started exploding."

"These 'friends' of yours...who are they exactly?"

asked Trina.

"I'm not really a big fan of labels," said Michelle.

"Mobsters?" asked Trina.

"Well, no. Not quite."

"Then what? Government? Spies?" asked Darren.

"They just... They keep an eye on things," said Michelle.

"Under whose authority?" asked Trina, getting impatient.

"It's not like that, from what I understand."

"What are you talking about?" said Trina.

"Just forget it. The point is, they're friends. Not enemies," said Michelle. "If it helps, think of them as sort of the Science Police."

"Science Police?" asked Darren. "Are you serious?"

"Yeah, they...you know, they make sure shit doesn't get too out of hand. They keep an eye on what's going on in the world, and make sure there are no major science-related catastrophes."

"They seem to be doing a great job," said Trina.

"Yeah, well, nobody's perfect, right?" said Michelle. "Look, they're on our side for this, and they're going to help us take care of the big green goblin out there. So unless you have any better ideas..."

"We haven't even heard this one yet," said Darren.

"Fair enough. So here it is. They figure this isn't a job for two or three people. This is a job for a few dozen, maybe close to a hundred people. But I'm talking a very select group. They figure we need to round up everyone who lost their phantom limbs to Dr. Rains, and we need to come together as a group to defeat this thing. Together, we can take our limbs back."

"Okay, so more than just a few people. Big deal," said Trina. "The entire city's police force is out there fighting this thing as we speak. Firefighters too. And the National Guard. Not to mention who knows how many civilians. What's a hundred more people?"

"Like I said, it's a very select, special group of people. You ready, Darren?" asked Michelle.

"Still a little fuzzy on the details here," he said.

"I don't have them all yet myself," said Michelle. "But these guys know what they're doing. They may work behind the scenes, so to speak, but I trust them. Besides, what other choice do we have?"

Darren sighed. "Okay. Whatever we need to do. That thing has my arm, and it's wrecking my city."

"Okay. Trina, feel free to make yourself at home," said Michelle.

"Wait, what?" Trina said, taken aback.

"I said make yourself at home. It's probably best to just stay in, lay low, ride this out, et cetera. With any luck, we'll be back before too long."

"What are you talking about? I'm going with you!" Trina said. She was getting more and more upset.

"Sorry, sweets. This is a war for the wounded, and you still have all your limbs," Michelle said, winking at Trina.

Darren stood up, ready to go along for the ride, whatever that ride might be.

"I think we've just gotta roll with this, hon," Darren said to Trina. "I don't totally know what I'm getting myself into, but I'm guessing you'll be safer staying here."

"Maybe," said Trina. "You be careful. I want you coming back in one piece."

Trina walked over to Darren and gave him a big hug. Then she placed her hands on his cheeks, looked deep into his eyes, and kissed him square on the lips.

"For luck," she said. Something inside Darren fluttered. He smiled.

Michelle smiled too, then rolled over to the window, opened it, and leaned out. "Hank? Whaddya say? Piggy-back ride?"

Darren was in a daze. The accumulated stress of the last several days had taken a toll, and his mind finally let it take hold of his body. He was exhausted, and struggling to pay attention. He had no idea how long Hank had been driving, or where they had gone. He only came to this realization as they pulled into what looked like an auto body shop, and the reinforced metal door closed down behind them.

"Wake up, stud. We're here," said Michelle, half-turned around in the front passenger seat of the Humvee. Hank had exited the vehicle and disappeared, only to return a moment later with a rolling office chair. He helped Michelle slide out and onto it.

Darren got out too. "So just where *is* here?" he asked.

Michelle whispered "Not completely sure. This isn't exactly what I was expecting."

Hank rolled Michelle across the room, through a door, and down a dimly-lit hallway. Darren followed. A moment later, they entered a predominantly dark room. The corner closest to the door was lit by a single low-wattage overhead light, but beyond that was darkness.

From somewhere in that darkness, a voice spoke.

"It was a bit of kismet, Michelle, when you reached out to us," it said. "You see, we had been trying to find you, and here, you called us. Funny how sometimes the best way to find something is to simply stop looking."

"Who's there?" Michelle asked into the void. The voice was male, but unfamiliar.

A dramatic silence hung in the space for a moment. Then a figure stepped forward, out of the darkness but still barely visible in the dim light. He removed a pair of long black rubber gloves.

"Greetings," the man said. He was tall and thin, with shock-white hair that seemed to explode in a horseshoe from the back of his head. He was dressed the part of a scientist, wearing a lab coat not too different from the one Dr. Rains used to wear, except this one was white and had no sleeves.

The dark room had a bit of an echo, leading Darren to think it was rather sizable. "My name is Dr. Franz," the man said from a distance, "and I've been anxious to meet you both." He extended his arm for a handshake. It stretched, like taffy, all the way from the center of the room to where Darren and Michelle were standing. They both shuddered. Things hadn't gone too well since their last encounter with a scientist. Neither of them spoke.

"I'll try not to take your reaction personally. I'm told you're the last two patients of a Dr. Griffin Rains. Is that correct?" He paused for a response that didn't come as he stepped toward them, his arm retracting back to its original, more socially acceptable length. "Well, yes, of course that's correct.

"Listen, I certainly understand any hesitation or apprehension you might be feeling at the moment. But unfortunately time is not on our side. You've no doubt noticed the little problem we have downtown? You know, the Giant Green Wrecking Machine?

"Well, I and my associates had been keeping an eye on Dr. Rains and this little experiment of his. We just didn't realize exactly what his endgame was, or that he would be mobilizing it quite so soon. Otherwise we would have tracked you both down a bit earlier.

"This 'SuperGhost' of his is clearly out of control, I'm sure you'd both agree. And something needs to be done about it."

"Obviously," said Michelle, finally finding her voice.

"Well, we've been working on something. In fact, we think we have a solution, and we'd like you both to be a part of it. Actually, we need you to be a part of it."

"What exactly did you have in mind?" asked Darren.

"I'll show you. Allow me to introduce you to some colleagues you may never have known you had. You see, Dr. Rains was a busy man, acting as a pseudo-therapist to nearly every amputee in the area. Mr. Henderson here lost both of his arms in the stands of a particularly violent baseball game. And Ms. Ramirez, beside him, lost a leg at Celery Fest three years ago."

"I remember hearing about that," said Darren. But neither he nor Michelle could see who Franz was referring to. The room was still very dark. The only logical assumption was that there were others in the room with them.

"You see, I've assembled all of Dr. Rains' former patients, all in one place, so that we can all work together to take down that horrid SuperGhost of his. Hank, would you get the lights?"

Hank brushed past Darren and stepped behind him to flip the switch on the wall, but Dr. Franz beat him to it, stretching his arm across the room again, winding around the edge of the wall, and flicking the switch up a second before Hank got to it.

"Little joke," said Franz, winking.

As the fluorescent tubes above flickered and came to life, a series of voices—male and female, young and old—each took their turn to say hello. When the room became illuminated, everything became apparent.

They were in an enormous warehouse, now aglow with artificial light. All of Dr. Rains' former patients were now present before Darren and Michelle. All in one mass, at least thirty feet tall. Maybe more.

It was a gigantic sphere of flesh, stitched and fused together, a massive ball made from the still-living bodies of amputees, all of whom were now willing to literally come together in an effort to defeat the SuperGhost.

The bulk of it was a curved cluster of torsos, hips, and faces—a heaving patchwork mass of flesh, wriggling with what must have been a couple hundred arms and legs, sprouting in all directions, like cilia, or sun rays in a child's drawing. Bodies had been fused together, sewn into a monstrous ball of multicolored skin, resembling something like a millipede curled up into something relatively spherical. It was like a small planet made of people.

Darren, agape, marveled at it, as the giant ball rolled toward them slowly, each hand and foot taking its turn to support a share of the thing's weight. He spotted a couple divots near what was now the top of the flesh-sphere.

After having seen the SuperGhost, both on television and firsthand, he imagined that, yes, something as wild as this might be the only shot they had to defeat Rain's creation.

"Are you fucking insane?" asked Michelle. "Hank, you left out a few details here, buddy."

"Science is a crazy thing, you know?" said Franz. "As soon as we realized that Dr. Rains had put his plan into motion, we began putting our own plan into place. Granted, it's a little rough around the edges—we haven't had much time to iron out the wrinkles—but, well, here we are." Franz paused. "How else do you fight a massive collaboration? With a collaboration of your own."

"Collaboration? More like abomination," said Michelle.

"It won't work without you," Franz said. "We really do need you. Both of you."

"Join us!" chanted the clustered crowd behind Franz. "We need you!" It sounded far more menacing than was probably intended. Most of the faces sewn into the surface of the thing seemed to be smiling and peaceful, but still retained an essence of determination.

"Darren, wouldn't you like to know what it's like to have your right arm back? Maybe a few extras? And Michelle, wouldn't you like to run again? Think of the speeds you could attain with two hundred legs. This is a chance. Not only to save the city, and possibly the world, but a once-in-a-lifetime chance to reclaim something that circumstance took from you along the way. We need an UltraHuman to fight a SuperGhost."

"UltraHuman?" Michelle said, laughing. "Seriously? What a dumb fucking name."

"We're open to suggestions, if you're willing to help." said the doctor.

"I don't know," Michelle said, shaking her head a bit. I look at this thing, and I just think...Meatball."

"Joiiinnn usssss!"

Michelle woke up, groggy. She wanted to roll over and continue sleeping, but neither of these things was possible. Not only was she now attached to several dozen other people, but there was important work to be done.

"Crazy, huh?" said Darren. His face was just a few feet to the right of Michelle's. "But desperate times call for desperate measures, as they say."

"I guess so."

"How are you feeling?" asked a voice from the underside of the ball of flesh they were now a part of.

"I don't even know how to respond to that," said Michelle. "I can't believe I'm doing this."

"Yeah, well, like you said, what other choice do we have?" said Darren. "We could sit back and let that thing destroy our world, or we can fight back. With any luck, we can save the city and get our phantom limbs back, and maybe, just maybe, get back to something resembling normal life."

Dr. Franz stepped into view. "Okay, folks. Rise and

shine!" The ball shifted a bit, and rose up on a few pairs of hands and feet.

"Obviously we've had to do some rearranging, for logistical purposes. Michelle, you'll notice your arms are there, and there. And Darren, your arm is on the left there. No, a bit south of where you're looking. Yes. And you probably won't be able to see your legs, but if you concentrate, you should be able to feel them moving.

"Okay. Now, we've got one more step to get through before showtime." Dr. Franz pulled a bundle of wires from a table, and moved toward the human sphere.

"Surely it's going to be difficult for so many minds and bodies to coordinate their movements," he said. He began placing suction cups on each forehead, stretching and curling his arms around the sphere as necessary, like a pair of giant snakes. A few moments later, each face was connected to the rest by a series of thin multicolored wires. The network braided together and trailed off toward a giant machine on the wall, something with a million flashing lights and buttons. Something that belonged in a movie, thought Michelle.

"So we've decided it's going to be necessary to link you all together, mentally. I've decided it would be best to keep one male brain and one female brain active, so that the two can control both the male and female parts of the assemblage, and also work in tandem, for balance. See if you can guess whom I've chosen."

Michelle and Darren looked at each other as best they could, given their now-limited neck movement. They nodded at each other, as if to say "Okay. Let's go."

"Darren and Michelle, together you'll have total

control over the entire structure. Michelle, you've got the females, and Darren, you have the males. The fact that you know each other already helps establish the link between you. The rest should be automatic, as we're introducing a suggestion to everyone else's brains."

"Like hypnotism?" asked Michelle.

"Similar, but more along psychic lines. Also, keep in mind you have a low-level electrical charge running inside you at all times. Surely you've seen the lightning inside the SuperGhost. The beast only becomes solid when there's enough current running through it. This should be enough so that whenever you make contact with it, you'll actually *make contact*, and not pass through it."

"How's this all work?" asked Darren.

"Do you really think we have time for details now? Since I put you both under for the attachment procedure, the SuperGhost has destroyed a-whole-nother section of the city. It's morning now."

"Did you really just say *'a-whole-nother'*?" said Michelle. "You know that's not actually a word, right? I mean, I thought you were a smarty-pants scientist."

"Let's not get bogged down with grammar, shall we? As I said, time is of the essence."

"Fine. Let's do this."

Dr. Franz waved a hand to Hank, who was standing across the room, near a switch on the wall. Hank hesitated for a second, expecting another trick from the doctor and his rubber arms, but it didn't happen. The doctor signaled, and Hank threw the lever. Then every eye on the Meatball rolled backward. A handful of sparks jumped from the machine on the wall. After a few seconds, it was done.

"That's it," said Dr. Franz. "Now focus, you two. If you concentrate, you should be able to feel every limb of the structure. And you should be able to feel each other inside your minds."

It was true, thought Darren. He could feel dozens of arms and legs, and the ability to control them. He could feel Michelle in his head too. It wasn't an overwhelming sensation—just a presence. A link.

"You feel it?" he asked her.

"Uh-huh. You ready to do this?" she replied.

Darren nodded.

Wild as the idea was, Dr. Franz seemed less like a mad scientist than Rains had to Darren. Somehow, this could work, he thought.

"Good. Let's go get that fucker," said Michelle.

The Meatball rolled forward, slowly at first.

The warehouse door rose like a stage curtain, and the ball of flesh picked up speed. Dr. Franz smiled, and walked over to Hank. They stood side by side, watching as the Meatball rolled through the massive doorway, ready for the performance of a lifetime. Franz nudged Hank in the ribs with a rubbery elbow.

"See? *Science is fun!*" he said.

Hours had passed, and the SuperGhost was still a whirling, green cloud of chaos, alternately passing and smashing its way through buildings, abandoned vehicles, and public sculpture. It had continued its spiral path through the city, destroying virtually everything in its path. Cars and buildings were still burning. People were still screaming, running for their lives, taking cover wherever they could. The police still had no control over the thing. Bullets and nets were useless. Roadblocks were futile.

The SuperGhost was joined by a pair of sidekicks now—two smaller assemblages, one a series of arms and legs that looked like a starfish, and the other a pair of legs attached by an arm, resembling a model of Stonehenge.

The trio was bearing down on an apartment complex when the Meatball rolled up onto a pile of wreckage, like a sunrise on the horizon.

The Meatball screamed from all of its mouths at once. The voice was a hybrid of all its parts and it echoed off the sides of the buildings that had yet to be knocked over.

"SuuuperrrGhooossst!"

The monster stopped for a moment, and turned to face the ball of flesh. The lightning inside it faded momentarily, and an air of calm momentarily blanketed the scene.

"We've come for you," announced the Meatball. "Not only have we come to save our city, but we've come to reclaim our phantom limbs. Let's stop this madness. Give it up, scrap heap!"

The SuperGhost took a step toward the mound on which the Meatball was perched, waving its dozens of phantom arms at length, like a cobra displaying its hood, as if to give the appearance of something even bigger than its already massive size. The pair of tentacles sprouting from its neck wiggled like a funny cartoon mustache, then gestured at the ball like a pair of beckoning fingers.

The Meatball screamed again, and launched an attack, rolling down from the pile of concrete and broken walls. Using a pair of twisted steel girders like tracks on a ramp, the ball of flesh launched itself into the air, in the direction of the ghost-beast. Seeing this, the SuperGhost went blank a second before impact, choosing to let the human monster pass through it and crash to the ground.

But Dr. Franz's concept proved to be valid, and the electrical current within the Meatball worked. It was enough of a charge to keep the ghost solid upon impact. The giant beasts collided, and the SuperGhost was knocked backward into the apartment building it had been a moment away from destroying anyway.

After the collision, the Meatball rolled over to the ghost, now lying on its back, partially embedded in the side of the building.

"You've got a piece of each of us. And we want them back." A half dozen arms reached out from the flesh-ball, and attempted to claw at the ghost. "You belong to us!"

The Meatball reached out to tear the SuperGhost apart. If the ghost could be separated again into its individual phantom limbs, the horror laying waste to the city would surely come to an end.

Without the psychic control of its master, the Super-Ghost was a twisted knot of anxiety. All the tingling sensations the amputees once felt were now connected into one ghostly form, and the only way that form could ease its own discomfort was to lash out. It knew only to destroy.

The SuperGhost lunged away from the clawing arms of the Meatball, and jumped across the street, landing atop a pile of crumpled cars. The lightning inside it exploded, and the ghost roared up into the air. Sparks flecked from its hundreds of fingertips.

The Starfish and Stonehenge flanked the Super-Ghost, then floated up into two of its hands. Suddenly the SuperGhost looked even more like a warrior. It struck a battle stance, cocked back the arm holding the Starfish, and threw it at the Meatball.

The Starfish spun through the air like a five-pointed Japanese throwing star. The ghost-limbed shuriken struck the Meatball with a flash of electricity, and wounded the flesh, nearly severing one of its many arms. But it didn't stick. Instead, it spun back through the air to the Super-Ghost's side, like a boomerang, ready to be tossed again.

The Meatball recovered quickly, and reset its stance.

Across the street, the SuperGhost was also ready for more. It held the Stonehenge experiment in one hand, grasping it around the ankles of both legs. Then, letting one of them fall loose, it began spinning the Stonehenge structure like a pair of nunchaku, two phantom legs connected by an arm.

The Meatball's eyes widened, its Darren-Michelle hybrid mind recognizing the danger. But it had to press forward. It rolled up another hill of wreckage, and prepared to launch itself at the SuperGhost again. It did so with force, rolling down the heap along a sheet of somehow-unbroken glass, then pitched itself into the air, shooting straight for the SuperGhost. The green monster swung its leggy nunchucks at the skin-ball, but did so erratically, and missed it completely, like a batter fanning at a curveball.

The Meatball managed to turn itself in mid-air, and strike the SuperGhost with a series of machine gun punches from a dozen arcing fists. The ghost fell backward again, while the Meatball landed and rolled easily out of harm's way.

It launched itself at the SuperGhost once more, and struck again with an equal number of kicks. Each strike was enhanced by the electrical current within both behemoths. The SuperGhost glowed fiercely with every shot. Though it did act stunned, it didn't seem to take any true damage from the Meatball's onslaught.

"Give up, SuperGhost! We can do this all day!"

The SuperGhost took a giant step back and threw the Starfish-shuriken again. This time, a green arm stuck in the side of the Meatball, piercing deep into the flesh of a man's chest, settling inside a pectoral muscle. Lightning flashed from the center of the Starfish, and the Darren-Michelle mind sizzled with pain. The ghostly hand seemed to want to dig further into the chest and tear out its heart. The Meatball screamed with all of its mouths, a chorus of agony. It shook the shuriken-ghost loose, though, and prepared for the next attack.

In the distance, a car horn sounded. Tires screeched as a familiar Humvee rounded the corner, crashing into an already crashed car. As usual, Hank and his sunglasses were behind the wheel.

The passenger door shot open, and Trina jumped out. "Darren! Michelle!" she screamed.

"You might have to address it as 'Meatball'," said Dr. Franz from the back seat. Trina didn't hear him.

The Meatball turned sideways, so that Darren and Michelle's faces could be seen by Trina. Trina was waving her arms to get its attention. She was yelling, but the Meatball couldn't understand a word through all the sounds of chaos in the area.

The ball of flesh rolled itself closer to Trina, and she repeated herself. "Happee Freeze! The ice cream factory! Over there! Push it that way!"

The Meatball saw what she was talking about, but didn't understand the logic.

"There's still power there, and a backup system! Come on! Push that green bastard to the ice cream factory!" Darren had always trusted Trina. Michelle could feel that, and she went along with it. The Meatball spun back toward the SuperGhost. Trina ran back to the car.

A barrage of rolling strikes followed, each one of them charged with electricity. The Meatball became a tsunami of fists and feet, backing the SuperGhost up with each shot. In a matter of minutes, they had arrived at the Happee Freeze factory.

Hank had been able to dislodge the vehicle from the crash, and drove over. Trina jumped out again, though she knew she could offer no physical support.

"The new freezer!" yelled Trina. "Head for the new freezer!" And the Meatball, trusting in her, did as requested. Trina had been right—it was the size of a domed stadium, with a pair of unnecessarily gigantic doors.

The Meatball spun in place for a moment, building up speed and momentum, then unloaded a single lightning-charged shot at the SuperGhost, knocking the monster backward into the factory's brand new massive storage freezer. The ball of flesh rolled in after it, ready to throw another powerful shot. Trina ran up behind, and threw a switch on the wall, causing the enormous doors to close and lock.

The Meatball began to spin again, as puffs of cold breath escaped its many mouths. But it didn't have to strike. With the freezer door closed, the already frigid temperature quickly dropped further, and the electricity inside the SuperGhost soon flickered, weakened, then faded to nothing as a film of frost began to form on both of the giants.

The Meatball's arms and legs began to quiver, feeling the cold take effect, stiffening its many limbs.

The SuperGhost shook too, but more violently. And then, the sound of ice crackled inside the freezer. The ghost stopped moving, and something shattered.

One after another, the phantom limbs broke their connections, and floated softly to the ground, shrinking to their original sizes in the process. Seconds later, the SuperGhost lay in pieces on the frozen floor of the Happee Freeze factory's new stadium-sized freezer.

Having heard the sound from outside, Trina pressed a button on the wall, then opened a small, human-sized door, and entered.

The Meatball turned slowly, shivering, and spoke in its hybrid voice. "How?" was all it said.

Trina smiled, exhausted. "Rains was a genius, no doubt. But like some other smart-heads I've known, he occasionally lacked common sense." She rubbed her hands together, blew hot air into one of them, then used it to pull something from her pocket—a wrinkled, spent tube of Dr. Rains' ConnECTO. "That dummy printed instructions on these things, like he was gonna sell the stuff at a hardware store or something."

"Huh?" asked the Meatball, and rolled a few feet closer to Trina.

"Always read the fine print, my friend." She held the tube up high, and pointed to the label. "Right here, in all caps. *'DO NOT FREEZE'*."

"So yeah, I've been training for a while now, thanks to these," said Michelle, gesturing down to her phantom legs, glowing green. She had metal bands strapped around the ends of her stumps, and each had a tiny power pack, and a prong hanging past the edge of her physical form, ensuring that just enough electricity found its way to the phantom limbs to keep them solid at all times.

"A couple more months, I think, and I'll be able to compete again," she said. "I just signed up for a 5K."

"Wow. That's amazing," said Trina, seated to her right. "Looks like your scars are healing nicely too," she said, referring to Michelle's neck, one of the areas of her body that had been briefly fused to the other members of the Meatball.

The hundred or so people filling the high school auditorium were all smiles. They were all amputees, many of them former members of the phantom limb support group Trina had dragged Darren to all those months ago. And they had all been a part of the Meatball that helped defeat the SuperGhost. They were like one big family now.

Everyone was happy. They all had their phantom limbs back, all had metal straps with power packs that kept their limbs solid. Everyone felt whole again.

Even Sexy the Sexopus was there, floating inside an aquarium on wheels. His two phantom tentacles were attached to the outside of the tank. Using psychic power, he was able to control them and grab physical objects outside the aquarium.

"Where's Darren?" Michelle asked.

"Oh, he's on his way," said Trina. "He called a little while ago to let me know he got held up at the site."

Just then, Darren walked through one of the side doors of the auditorium, preceded by the soft green glow of his phantom arm. He was still wearing his hardhat. He approached Trina, who stood up and gave him a long kiss on the lips. They looked each other in the eyes for a moment, and Darren ran a finger down her blue streak of hair.

"Hey babe," she said. She brushed some dust off his shoulder, and wrapped an arm around his waist.

The crowd noticed he had walked in, and cheered.

"How's it going, big guy?" asked Michelle, standing up on her phantom legs.

"Couldn't be better," he said. "I've got my arm back, and I'm doing what I love, helping to rebuild the city. How about you?"

"Everything's back on track," she said.

"Actually, I think there's one small detail that could make things just a little better for all of us," said Trina. She motioned across the room. Two men stepped out into the hall, and returned a minute later, rolling in a big freezer on wheels.

"Ladies and gentlemen," Trina announced, "Happee Freeze Ice Cream is proud to introduce our newest flavor, Phrozen Phantom Phudge! Enjoy!"

Darren's eyes lit up. *"Mmm...Chocolate..."*

THE SCIENCE FAIR

"We're going to be late, sweetie! Let's go!"

There was a thunderous burst of sound above. Then, seconds later, Griffin raced down the stairs, his feet thudding against the carpeted steps in rapid machine gun fire. The noise startled his mother, even though she was the one who had beckoned.

He plodded across the living room, toward the front door of their home and dropped to the floor, where he stuffed his feet into a pair of sneakers—which, just this week, had started to border on being too small. Maybe he was hitting his own growth spurt, like his brother had a few months prior.

"Okay, come on, let's get in the car."

"Wait, where's—"

"He wanted to take the bus," Griffin's mother responded. "Which may have been a good decision, because he's probably at school already. But if we don't leave right this instant, we're going to be late, so *let's goooooooo.*"

As Griffin stood back up, his mother handed him his jacket and a granola bar with one hand while guiding him through the front door with the other. It had been a hectic morning, leaving no time for a proper breakfast. But they couldn't afford to be late today.

•

Griffin stared out the passenger side window of his mother's car, but wasn't paying attention to the passing scenery. He was lost in his own thoughts as the news played from the radio in the background.

He usually rode the bus to school with his brother, but this morning was different. Today was the annual Science Fair. Without any help from his parents (after all, they were busy people and not exactly inclined to the sciences), Griffin Rains had assembled what he believed to be his greatest achievement yet. Several weeks of dedicated work had gone into it, and he had dreamt about this day every night for some time. He was excited to premiere his project for his teachers and classmates, and bask in their inevitable praise and adulation. It was going to be a good day.

Griffin's father had helped him pack everything into bins and boxes, and load it all into the car the night before. His father always left for work prior to the sun rising, so he had wished his son good luck when he slammed the back gate shut and kissed his cheek goodnight. He said he would do his best to stop by the school the next day, but that work might keep him from doing so. That was an old story, as far as Griffin was concerned—one he was used to hearing his entire life.

He scratched behind his ear and ran a hand through the hair on the side of his head. Several loose strands came out between his fingers. He brushed them on his leg, then scratched an itch just beneath his armpit.

"Everything okay?" his mother asked. "Did you put

your deodorant on this morning?"

Griffin nodded, and continued staring out the window at nothing in particular. His mother shifted her focus back to the road.

She was driving fast. Very fast. Griffin hadn't noticed at first, but he eventually became aware of her weaving around other cars, narrowly squeaking through yellow lights at virtually every intersection, and generally standing on the gas pedal. The next thing he knew, they were pulling into the school parking lot.

"Where do we need to be, the gym?" his mother asked.

"Yeah. I think so."

Griffin hated the gym. It stank of industrial-strength cleaning supplies covering the stench of stale sweat. He felt much more at home in the classroom, or in the makeshift laboratory his father had helped him set up in the basement at home. It wasn't much—just a table and a metal cabinet, some test tubes and beakers. He worked on some of his experiments there. Others he toyed with in the privacy of his bedroom.

His brother, on the other hand, loved the gym. He was the athlete of the family. They were twins, but polar opposites. His brother was the outgoing, popular one at school, while Griffin was quiet, preferring science and math to just about everything else.

His mother brought the car to a quick stop near the side entrance to the school, although she couldn't remember the door's proximity to the gymnasium. She darted out of the driver's side, and opened the back hatch before Griffin had even undone his seat belt. He'd had some late nights recently, making final preparations on his project, and they were catching up with him. The objects whizzing past the window of the car during the ride had made him realize this. He felt groggier now than when he first woke up.

The gymnasium turned out to be at the opposite end of the school from where they had gotten out, but rather than get back in and drive around, Griffin's mother decided to just load everything onto the red metal hand truck her husband had loaded into the car and wheel it through the central hallway as quickly as she could. Griffin grabbed a black plastic milk crate filled with the signs and charts he planned to display, and followed his mother. It was the lightest part of the load.

Mr. Nakajima, Griffin's science teacher, was standing at the entrance to the gym.

"Good morning, Griffin," he said, making a mark on his clipboard. He was happy to see his young student. He saw a lot of potential in the boy. "And you must be Mrs. Rains."

"Yes. Hello there," she said with a friendly smile. "Are we in the right place?"

"Absolutely," the teacher replied. "Follow me and I'll show you to your spot, Griffin."

The gym was already abuzz with students and parents. Griffin chuckled to himself, as he could instantly tell which projects were the work of his fellow students and which were the work of his fellow students' *parents*. He assumed the judges would be able to tell the difference too.

Mr. Nakajima strolled through the aisles, leading them to Griffin's assigned table location. Griffin sensed that the teacher wasn't moving fast enough for his mother, who still had to get to work herself that morning, but they arrived, eventually, at his spot in the far corner of the gym. A six-foot long table stood inside the lines of tape on the floor that demarcated each student's space. A plain black tablecloth covered the table, and a piece of paper with "Rains, G." printed on it sat on top, secured with another strip of tape.

"All the way back *here*, huh?" Griffin's mother said under her breath. She had hoped her son would be featured more prominently, or at least more centrally, though she understood the table selection was random and there could be no favoritism. But he was such a smart boy. She didn't understand half of what he did about science, and he was still so young. He deserved to have his brilliant mind noticed by his teachers. Perhaps it would be. Perhaps this science fair was the start of a new chapter for her son. She dreamed of the possibilities. Maybe, a few years from now, he would even get a university scholarship.

"Well, let me or one of the other teachers know if you need anything, Griffin," Mr. Nakajima said. "And good luck!" Then, tucking his clipboard under one arm, the teacher traced his steps back to the gym's entrance.

"Thanks," Griffin said softly, too late for the teacher to hear. He set his milk crate down and scratched his side.

"You sure you're okay?" his mother said, reaching toward her son. "You're not getting a rash, are you? Here, let me take a look."

"Mom, stop!" Griffin said. There was some force behind the words, but he stifled it as best he could. "I'm fine. I just had an itch."

"Okay, okay. Here, tell me what I can do. I need to get to work, but I can help for a few minutes. I'll follow your lead."

"I'll be fine," Griffin said. "Go ahead."

His mother slid the hand truck out from beneath the stack of boxes and bins it carried. "You're sure? I can stay for a few minutes."

"I'm sure. I need to spend a few minutes thinking about *how* I want to set things up before I actually set things up anyway."

His mother smiled and gave him a kiss on the cheek.

"Okay then. Good luck," she said. "I'll be by after work." Then she grabbed the hand truck and exited the gymnasium quickly. In the hallway, she noticed something in the wheels starting to make a dinging sound.

•

Griffin, and every other science fair participant had been given until the end of the first period to get their displays set up. The fair itself wasn't until the end of the day. In the interim, a trio of judges would survey each project and tally their preliminary scores, which they would follow up on later with a few brief questions for each student.

Griffin felt anxious throughout the day. Normally he was extremely focused during his science and math classes, and fairly engaged in his other subjects as well, but the science fair dominated his mind today, and he stayed quiet through each period, vigorously bouncing his knees, attempting to will the clock to spin forward with his mind. *If only he had a time machine.*

That afternoon's gym class was held outside for obvious reasons, and a game of flag football had been organized. Griffin hated sports, but at least there was a version of this game with reduced brutality.

His brother was on the opposite team, and had already scored two touchdowns in the first ten minutes of play. Although Griffin was unenthusiastic about being involved in the game himself, he was happy for—and proud of—his brother. It looked as if they were both going to have a successful day.

Suddenly Griffin was slammed into from behind. His body launched forward, and his face ended up in the dirt. A small group of boys laughed hysterically. Griffin recognized them as being from the football team—the real football team—but didn't know any of them well. *"Nerd!"* came from one of their mouths as they jogged back to the line of scrimmage, but Griffin didn't see whose.

"Alright, alright," said the gym teacher. "No tackling today, you crazy kids." But there was no further reprimand. From the ground, Griffin actually saw the teacher chuckling, and knocking his elbow into one of the offending boys, as if to say "good one".

His brother helped him up off the ground. "These boneheads," he said. "You okay?"

Griffin nodded, then picked a piece of grass off his bottom lip. He brushed the dirt off his shirt and arms. He scratched his side and realized one of his elbows was bleeding.

He decided to go sit on the sideline, regardless of whether or not it was allowed. But the teacher didn't even seem to notice. Griffin sat there, stewing, watching the other kids continue the game. He considered racing back out onto the field himself and tackling as many other kids as he could, but decided against it, figuring he would only end up more hurt himself in the process, then potentially rewarded with a detention. It wouldn't be worth it. So he decided to hold off. He'd get back at them another way, another day.

Griffin went to the nurse instead of his next class, to have his elbow looked at. After the wound area was cleaned, it didn't look half as bad as it had outside.

•

The science fair officially started during the last period of the school day. Each student with a project was allowed to leave halfway through the second to last period, to attend to their displays and make sure everything was in order.

When the bell for last period sounded, a wave of students poured into the gymnasium. Griffin stood in his corner booth, waiting for his classmates to approach. Surely they would be enthralled by his findings, enamored with the brilliance of his mind. This was undoubtedly his ticket to popularity.

But most of the students couldn't be bothered to care at all. A few walked past Griffin's booth without even a glance in his direction. *How strange*, he thought. He came out from behind the table to take a fresh look at the display and make sure nothing was misplaced or arranged in the wrong order. It wasn't. Everything was set up perfectly.

"Hey, uhh, check out this frog," he said to several girls walking past, but they only gave disgusted looks and shuffled out of the area immediately.

To say he was disappointed was an understatement. He had expected to make a splash, but, halfway through the period, not a single student had approached his display, let alone asked about his project.

Then, across the gym, he spotted the football players—the group of boys from earlier. If there was anyone he *didn't* want to approach his table, it was them.

"And next we have Griffin Rains," a high-pitched voice said. It was one of the judges. Griffin looked up and saw three adults step in front of his area—a man and two women. He recognized them as teachers, but they taught a grade ahead of his, so he didn't know any of them personally.

"*Regenerative Limbs*," one of the women said, reading aloud the title of his display, "*In Flatworms, Frogs, and... Humans?* Well, that's certainly an ambitious project."

Griffin smiled. Maybe this was the moment he had been waiting for.

"But in examining everything here," she continued, "your project appears to be *unfinished*."

It was like a punch to the gut. Griffin felt sick.

"What do you—" he said, dumbfounded.

"Your instructions were to develop a hypothesis and conduct an experiment to test a theory," the male judge said. "Do you have a hypothesis? If you do, it isn't displayed here."

The room began to spin. Griffin felt dizzy. He tried to speak, but nothing came out when he opened his mouth.

"This is just a bunch of charts, and a frog with two legs," the third judge said. "And I see nothing about relating this to human limb regeneration at all."

"Did you...actually *cut this frog's legs off?*" the man asked.

"Yes, well—"

"I'm sorry, Griffin, but I'm afraid we're going to have to rule your project incomplete," the first judge said. "There's no hypothesis here that's been tested, and apparently no experiment to judge. As it is, this simply isn't a proper science fair project. I'm sorry."

The judges stepped away, moving their frowning faces to the next table down the line. Griffin dropped down onto the plastic folding chair behind his display, his world now decimated.

Why hadn't he been able to speak? He had arguments to counter everything the judges had said to him. He leaned forward, arms crossed in front of his body, his elbows resting on his knees, one of them throbbing. He scratched his side vigorously, then smoothed the action into a soft rubbing motion. He felt the lump of flesh that was beginning to grow out from beneath his armpit. He could tell there was bone beneath it, exactly as he had expected.

He had wanted to tell the judges about that, about the experiments he had been conducting at home, *on his own body*, and the results he had seen so far. But his work wasn't as far along as he had hoped just yet. Still, he thought the display he had assembled was good enough. The seeds of the idea were there, *weren't they?* It was absolutely feasible that humans could regrow lost limbs, or, in his case, grow *extras*. He scratched his side again. It was only a matter of time. Soon, maybe a few more weeks from now, his third arm would be fully formed. He would find those judges then and show them what he had done. They would be amazed. They would probably change the results of the science fair and award him the gold medal, or at least give him a special trophy. He could see the gymnasium now, rearranged into a banquet for the award ceremony.

"What's up, nerd? How's the elbow?" The football players had made their way across the gym, and now stood before Griffin's display. He didn't respond.

Griffin glanced up at the clock and saw that the period was just about to end. These boys would probably have to run off to practice any minute. He tried to move the clock forward with his mind again, but was once again unsuccessful.

One of the boys threw a punch at Griffin's display, knocking one of the standing poster boards off the table.

"Whoa, check out this frog!" another one exclaimed, picking the creature up out of its glass enclosure. Two of the other kids suddenly swiped their hands across the table, knocking most of its contents to the floor. They all laughed.

Griffin didn't even flinch, though. He just sat and stared at them, fuming once again. He felt pressure on his side, as if he had a new hand clenching itself into a fist, just beneath the surface of his skin.

"We gotta go to practice, guys," one of the kids said, noticing the time. "Coach said he'd make us run extra laps if we're late again." Then he faced Griffin and said "I'm gonna keep this frog. Hope that's okay with you, nerd." The group walked away.

Griffin left the scattered mess as it was and walked outside to wait for his mom in the parking lot. He looked at all the other kids, and the teachers, and the handful of parents who were beginning to arrive at the school. They all seemed to be having fun.

But it turned out not to be the great day he was expecting for himself. He just wanted to go home, and maybe spend some time in his lab. Maybe he would double the amount of the concoction had had been injecting under his arm, to see if that accelerated the pace of his new growth. Maybe he would plot revenge.

He would show people, someday. He would show them the things he could accomplish. He would show them the vastness of his brilliance. He would *change the world.*

Someday.

ACKNOWLEDGEMENTS

First and foremost, I have to thank my wife Gina for her unending love and support, and for being the best Pancake Dance partner in the world.

Special thanks also go to Adam Cesare for his writing advice, encouragement, and friendship, and to Spike Marlowe for her wonderful suggestions and editorial wizardry on the original version of this book.

ABOUT THE AUTHOR

Scott Cole is a writer, artist, and
graphic designer living in Philadelphia.

He likes old radio dramas, old horror comics,
weird movies, cold weather, coffee, and a few other things too.

Find him on social media, or at www.13visions.com.

Made in the USA
Lexington, KY
10 November 2019

56691683R00092